PARAIG MacNEIL is a storyteller of ... the unbroken line of his *seannach...* ... ... in his ancient Highland dress, Paraig tells stories from memory of ancient Celtic heroes, clan legends, Jacobites, Highland Clearances and the Wars of Independence. These are all punctuated by verse, song, proverb, riddle and rhyme. He lives in Dunblane with his wife, Alison. More information about Paraig can be found at www.paraigmacneil.co.uk

In memory of Auld Davie Stewart

CONTENTS

Acknowledgements   ix

Foreword   xi

Introduction   xiii

Prologue

1   (Jarl) Henry Sinclair
2   James Gregory
3   John Arbuthnot
4   Alexander Selkirk
5   James Francis Edward Keith
6   Sir Hugh Dalrymple
7   Alexander Cruden
8   Robert Smith
9   John Witherspoon
10   Adam Smith
11   John Broadwood
12   Alexander (Secundus) Monro
13   James Watt
14   John Paul Jones
15   Helen Gloag
16   Thomas Smith
17   Sir John Sinclair
18   William Murdoch
19   Robert Burns
20   Alexander MacGillivray
21   Thomas Telford
22   Lachlan MacQuarrie
23   William MacLure
24   Sir Alexander MacKenzie
25   John Loudon McAdam
26   Alexander Wilson
27   Charles Macintosh
28   Sir James MacGrigor
29   Robert Stevenson
30   James Coats

31 Janet and James Keiller
32 Alexander Cumming
33 Sir John Ross
34 Andrew Ure
35 Sir David Brewster
36 Alexander Maconochie
37 Mary Fairfax Somerville
38 James Chalmers
39 John Ross (Cherokee)
40 Robert Napier
41 Sir William Drummond Stewart
42 James Gordon Bennett
43 David Douglas
44 James Bowman Lindsay
45 James Clark Ross
46 Alexander Shanks
47 John Pullar
48 Michael Nairn
49 Hugh Falconer
50 James Nasmyth

Appendix I   The Metrical Mirror   103

Appendix II   The Spirituality of *Brainheart*   108

Appendix III   Nova-riddles   116

Further Reading   119

Index   121

ACKNOWLEDGEMENTS

Whilst performing at a museum's festival in the Highlands in 2003, an idea came to me to invent some modern riddles and put them into rhyming form. Those riddles were to be about Scottish inventions. I believed that they might provide a fun way to raise an awareness of the age of innovation, but remain in keeping with the tradition of brain teasing. So, initially I wrote 20 rhyming riddles, and incorporated them into story-telling for upper-primary-school aged children. I launched this in the form of traditional storytelling, during the autumn of 2003 whilst visiting schools.

After this, I wrote another 21 rhyming riddles and again incorporated them into storytelling. The response was very positive. I have since baptised these riddles 'Nova-riddles'. Some of these are in Appendix III of this volume.

The idea then came to me that perhaps the innovators them-selves merited being eulogised in some kind of traditional format. I was inspired to think of Blind Harry's great epic poem, 'The Wallace'. Having been well acquainted with Harry's work, and realising that this was too good an idea to ponder over slowly, I went to work immediately. With the help of a biographical dictionary and the Internet, I diligently set to work.

By early 2004, the first draft was complete. But the real work was now to begin. After quite a few re-workings of those 2,000 lines and a further 16 months of chopping and changing, I completed this volume of *Brainheart*.

It was a challenging exercise for me in many ways, not least of all trying to work with a clapped-out old computer, and in an environment unsuitable for a would-be writer. However, Alison, my wife, was a great support to me, quite often walking around on eggshells, as I blazed new trails through my brain. Alison also helped by reading some of the earlier pieces out to me and rectifying errors in the text.

I would also like to thank the staff of both Dunblane and Stirling libraries for helping me to gain access to limited publ-ications. I would like to thank Margaret Bennett, folklorist, writer and singer, for her continued kind words of encourage-ment towards this venture, even from the beginning when the first drafts, though laced with enthusiasm, were in need of re-crafting. Thanks also go to Steve McGrail, freelance writer, for viewing it at various stages and for his comments.

My gratitude for continued viewing of various drafts go to Elspeth King of the Smith's Gallery, Stirling; Fiona Watson of Stirling University's Environmental History Department; and Alasdair Macrae, retired lecturer in English Studies, Stirling University, especially for his comments on punctuation. Also, my youngest sister (actress and playwright) who, although lives in London, was willing to view much of the work, and gave me valuable advice on assonance and alliteration. I would like to thank the late Davie Stewart of Dunblane for his continued encouragement and always handing me newspaper cuttings and features about Scotland's innovators, old and contemporary.

I would like also to express my gratitude to Gavin MacDougall of Luath Press, Edinburgh for enthusiastically embracing this idea from its inception.

Finally, I also have to thank years of exposure and practice of the ancient art of traditional storytelling, poetry and song (especially traditional Gaelic and Scots), which has provided for me, besides countless other things, a few hints about traditional rhetoric, and the many good people with whom I have been blessed enough to have had acquaintance within those fields.

Paraig MacNeil

FOREWORD

The idea of making an epic poem is one thing; carrying it out is quite another. That not only requires the bard's talent, skill, insight and imagination, but also passionate committment and stamina. Blind Harry's epic, 'The Wallace' stands as the classic, though we should not forget Zachary Boyd's colourful biblical 26,000 line epic, 'Zion's Flowers':

> ...*So Jacob made for his wee Josie*
> *A tartan coat tae keep him cosy...*

Since Boyd's death in 1653, however, nobody seems to have taken up the mantle for Scotland – not until Paraig MacNeil created *Brainheart* to celebrate Scotland's inventors.

Readers, listeners and reciters alike will love this inspirational, witty, catchy, amusing work. Because it's such fun, children will remember what they learn from it. And equally important, *Brainheart* will help nurture a healthier national pride, and boost confidence too often lacking in modern Scotland.

Margaret Bennett

Blind Harry, in the late 15th century, published and performed his great epic poem 'The Wallace' in rhyming couplets, depicting the life and times of the hero of the Wars of Independence, William Wallace. This poem was also, in recent times, interpreted for a worldwide audience on the big screen by the movie *Braveheart*.

Harry's work is a celebration of Wallace's heroism, military achievement and moral victory over the enemy. In its nature, it is a great epic, which is meant to be recited or declaimed episodically. Its purpose is to inspire, enthral, and lead the listener or reader to a sense of self worth through the achievements of the hero. Forensic fixations about 'the facts' should be laid aside by the listener or the reader, as the author is trying to impart greater truths.

Elspeth King, Introduction to *Blind Harry's Wallace*
(Luath Press, 1998)

Harry's epic poem (12,000 lines) that we now know as 'The Wallace' was based on the Latin Chronicles of Bishop Sinclair, the *Fechting Bishop*, who was with William Wallace throughout the Wars of Independence, plus stories of the hero that had been handed down through successive generations. The work was interwoven with fantastic imagery and was therefore propagandist in nature. Harry himself felt inadequate and unqualified to carry out such a task but did it because he saw a need for it and realised that no-one else could be bothered.

Seven hundred years have gone since the days of William Wallace. Since Blind Harry's work extolled the marshal virtues from those warlike ages, I feel that the time has now come to echo that work reflecting heroism with heroism of an equally important kind, which would stem from a more recent era of history, that is, the age of innovation.

Gaelic heroic poetry was balanced with marshal, moral, artistic and intellectual virtues being extolled. Here are some sample verses from the epic 'Lament to Rob Roy', as seen through the eyes of his grieving spouse:

Bu tu seabhag an t-sluaigh
  You were the falcon of the people
Ris an cainnte Rob Ruadh
  Who was called Rob Roy

'S math thig breacan mun cuairt a's claidheamh dhuit
  Well looked the tartan plaid round you and sword

Dh'fhalbh sealladh nan sul
  The eyesight has gone
'S stad an teanga a b'fhearr luth
  The most eloquent tongue has been stopped
'S tha an t-sluasaid's an uir a' feitheamh ort
  Now only the spade and the rough earth wait for you

Bha thu borb ann an stri,
  You were fierce in battle
Bha thu ciuin ann an sith,
  You were gentle in peace
Bu cheannard roimhe mile claimheamh thu
  The commander of a thousand swords were you

Bu bhoidheach sealladh do shiul
  Beautiful was the sight of your eye
Chan eil Morair no Diuc
  There is not a Lord or Duke
Air nach bhuinigeadh tu'n cuisibh seadhachais
  Who could defeat you in matters of intellect

This is a good example of how heroes were eulogised. The importance of being given to more sensitive pursuits in times of peace was held in high esteem by the people and the bards.

For the purpose of *Brainheart*, I have borrowed this concept but produced it in a different rhyming format. Wherefore 'The Wallace' would highlight the need of freedom from oppression, so would *Brainheart* mirror the more peaceable but equally beneficial gifts to all. 'The Wallace' (as interpreted by *Braveheart*) would represent what we as Scots did for ourselves, whereas *Brainheart* would reflect what we have given out to the world.

In short, both can complement each other. It could be likened unto the concept that rebuilding follows freedom's gain.

Scotland has long suffered the mockery of alien sectarian, social, and class division intrusions. This work is intended to be a light-hearted reflection and a token salutation to that un-self-conscious egalitarian attitude, inherent and visible in many Scots even to this day. Those values are still almost certainly traceable back to that ancient *stoc* of pre-sectarian, pre-denominational non-judgemental Celtic Christianity, which came some 1,500 years ago. Its mission mindedness halted the wars between Pict and Scot, uniting them under the doctrine of a god who breathed no hell-fire nor damnation, therefore no legacy of a fear of the future. This laid the foundation for this nation that we now call Scotland.

By highlighting this lesser-known age of heroism and the age of innovation in this very traditional style, I believe we might have a glimpse into the mirror of our true ancient selves. And perhaps reawaken or regenerate the possibilities within.

THE FORMAT

Although *Brainheart* is parallel with Harry's work and echoes the ethos of Gaelic hero poetry, the format is slightly different. 'The Wallace' was set in rhyming couplets in the form of 'iambic pentameter' (five iambic, or heart beats, to each line) which is also known as the 'hero' metre. For this work I felt that the iambic tetrameter (four iambic beats to each line) would be more appropriate, since it has a lighter feel, as has the whole subject matter. This metre would therefore be the same as that of Robert Burns's epic poem 'Tam o' Shanter' and Barbour's epic poem 'The Bruce'.

Based upon Gaelic poetry's ancient rhyming systems, I have developed a form of internal rhyme for epic verse, whereby each major vowel is marked rhythmically by the second stroke in each beat, by reflecting the matching vowel sounding in the corresponding line of the couplet, thereby mirroring the sound. I have baptised this the *Metrical Mirror* – see Appendix 1.

Another noteworthy difference is that although other characters are incidental in the couplets, Blind Harry narrated the deeds mostly of one hero, at one place, and at one time, whereas in this work, there are many heroes doing totally different things, at different places, and during different time periods in history, thus making the exercise much more concentrated.

Blind Harry produced 'The Wallace' in segments – volumes or books. My aim is to do likewise. Each volume should have a minimum of 2,000 lines each. The innovators in each volume should be set out as near as possible in chronological order from the date of their respective births.

Because each innovator is eulogised in 40 lines, this might also mean that each piece might be read or recited as one individual piece or as a component part of the whole in any order that the reader might choose, such as subject matter or in chronological order.

Whilst writing in verse of these great innovators, a common thread began to emerge which might connect them philosophically or spiritually. Just what was it that could make such a small nation produce so many geniuses so far out of proportion to its population? I began to conclude that it seemed to point back to our most ancient rights. My own observations, findings, opinions and conclusions are recorded in Appendix II.

My vision for this venture is that it might lead the readers to take a healthier but more objective look at their recent past in the light of the ancient past, gaining a better idea of where we have come from, and where we ought to be heading. This might inspire the reader to see in his or herself their true potential and see that light switch on again.

As we speak, there are Scots here in Scotland and around the world doing great and mighty things, yet often their inherent humility stymies them from receiving the proper credit.

Recent statistics seem to indicate that as many as 10,000 Scots per annum are quitting the country to find opportunity elsewhere. However, as I speak (March 2007) we, as a nation, are suffering from an uncontrollable alcohol and drug problem amongst the young. Our prisons are full of small-time offenders who continue to re-offend in order to feed their addictions. You will find the same problems in and amongst the Nez Perce Indians of Seattle, whose feelings of hopelessness have caused them to have an average life expectancy of 30 years of age! Incidentally, many of them are called MacDonald! It would appear that self-demeaning and self-destruction are partners.

We need to revive a healthy sense of national identity that is based again upon what we can give, not on what we can get. The time has come to end the 'it's all their fault' or 'it's all our fault' futile finger pointing. We need to re-throne dignity and self-worth and see beyond the dilemma that causes us to be slaves to the next pay cheque or mortgage repayment. A healthy, thriving nationalism must never be based on antipathy but on an ethical and ethnical self-respect. In short, we need to become a nation of visionaries once again. To quote the late Hamish Henderson in his flitting 'To Hugh MacDiarmid':

If we think all our ills come from 'ower the Border'
We'll never, but never, march ahead in 'guid order'.

THE PROLOGUE

Since the human race is of the one blood, prejudice against any people on the premise of genetic superiority would be a mockery of pure science and morality, leading to a warped perception of one's own nationality's worth.

It is my vision that Brainheart *will set out before the reader the story of innovators whose genius would have to be attributed to more than bloodline alone.*

Now that Scotland has regained some autonomy, the time is drawing near for the wounds of the past to heal, and to halt that self-blame culture that so often befalls a dying nation.

Glossary/Explication

LINE 3 'Twenty thousand moons' is approximately 16¼ centuries from whence the Scots (an elite royal warrior dynasty) expanded the kingdom of Dalriada from Ireland into Argyll, making the original Scots and Irish race as confirmed by recent DNA tests. I have used this American Indian term here (the moons) to empathetically draw a comparison between their plight and ours.

LINE 6 Anti-Scottish sleaze being perpetrated by Scottish writers is now endemic. The falcon sees all and kills at 80 mph.

LINE 17 The Scots of the modern world are comparable to the Greeks of the ancient world, contributing to the human race in the way of inventions, discoveries, explorations, medicines, communication, human rights, politics, etc.

LINE 21 Christian missionaries came with the original Scots, making Scotland probably the only nation actually founded upon Christianity, which the native Picts embraced readily. This Celtic Christianity would lead to the first ever human rights charter in 697 AD, the Cáin Adomnáin, followed by the first ever written legal constitution in the year 800AD, penned by the monks of Iona. Many other subsequent human rights movements have echoed these throughout the ages.

LINE 22 As evident by the current depressed state of the nation.

LINE 28 'Weft and warp' – a weaver's term for the yarns or threads being interwoven at right-angles to each other, e.g. for tartan.

LINES 29–33 Compare the brawn with the brain. See note on LINE 34 below.

LINE 34 In the Highlands, 1 May to 31 October was traditionally regarded as summertime, when the folk would migrate upwards to the mountain shielings (turf hut dwellings), where the young men would follow their heroic pursuits of tracking, droving, hunting and weapon training, whilst the young women and children would churn butter to make cheese, etc., in preparation for the approaching winter when the people would descend the hills with their cattle into the glens for the wintering. So from the end of October onwards, the indoor intellectual and native arts pursuits would follow, ie. storytelling, poetry, song, music, versification, etc. Therefore 'Mind's mould for mantle' represents the plaid and its outdoor heroic pursuits being seasonally replaced by the intellectual pursuits of the winter.

LINE 38 'Breaching rut' – the dilemma of uninformed national pride at loggerheads with the agony of self-hopelessness.

BRAINHEART: THE PROLOGUE

What ails us all at tunnel's end?
The day must dawn for us tae mend.
Can twenty thousand moons belie
What every founding truth here cries?
As falcons deftly, swiftly kill,   5
Let's quash or quell the quisling quill.
Now, dare I start by stating how
Our ancient heart and sacred vow
In wit or wisdom we can't hide,
Did give, forgive all, gear and guide.   10
In pairing rhyme, at metered pace,
Our nation's pride, let's re-embrace.
Let's break the noise of self-demeaning,
And praise the voice that's ever dreaming.
Oh hear me! faithful fellow Scot,   15
You clearly hae what hecklers sought.
Old Greeks' true mentored sons are you,
So, see yourself as others do!
Your fame has flown to far-flung corners,
But maimed at home through tiresome scorners.   20
Although from noble bonds begotten,
At home your soul is long forgotten.
There's scarce an ode that would declaim
Frae stage, grand court or couthy hame
The monumental bold and brave art   25
That Scots could better boast as Brainheart.
If mightier is pen than sword
Then write I will in weft and warp.
Apart frae claymores' clash in quarries,
And hardy hale hordes' flash swift forays   30
Wi' war-cries, plaided tartan tribesmen
O' brawn, lies brain with arts besides them.
'Twas shieling time the bold would battle.
On peat-lit nights, mind's mould for mantle.
So peat or coal lump, feed on flame,   35
To cheer or follow equal fame.
I'll fill your ears with coupled verses
Until yon breaching rut reverses.
So broach the barrel, sup and listen!
The story's partly just beginning.   40

1 (JARL) HENRY SINCLAIR 1345–1400

Henry Sinclair was born into a family with great power and prestige in Scotland, France and Norway. The Sinclairs were the Norman Earls of Rosslyn.

Henry married the daughter of the King of Norway, but after her death later remarried, producing 13 children. He had held a charter for Pentland and Rosslyn for Robert III of Scotland and was named Earl of Orkney and Lord of Shetland by the King of Norway, the power of which gave him considerable freedom.

With a fleet bigger than the Norwegian king's, he began on an epic adventure to the New World, a century before Christopher Columbus.

Glossary/Explication

LINE 1 Saint-Clair in Normandy was already half Norse. It is this language that his surname, Sinclair, comes from.

LINE 2 Rosslyn, now spelled Roslin, south of Edinburgh, is where the Templars have their graves. Sinclair held a barony there.

LINE 3 Robert III, King of Scots.

LINE 6 'Their' – Orkney and Shetland belonged to Norway at that time.

LINE 7 The responsibilities of his posts required ships and he started his own fleet, travelling between Norway, Orkney and Shetland, where he built two castles.

LINE 10 Robert III, King of Scots.

LINES 11–13 As Admiral of the High Seas for Scotland, his fleet numbered 13 ships, larger than the official fleet of King Eric of Norway.

LINE 17 On the conquest of the Faroe Isles, he met with the Venetian voyager Nicolo Zeno, and appointed him to be pilot and captain of his fleet. Nicolo Zeno told Henry a tale of fishermen, blown by storm to the New World, which highly intrigued Henry.

LINE 19 Zeno's Map was sent back to a third brother in Venice, called Carlo 'the Lion', as a testimony of this voyage.

LINE 21 By then he was appointed as Prince. He left from the Orkneys on his epic journey to America and it is this that I have focused on mostly here.

LINE 27 'Gooscap' – white god.

LINE 28 'Micmacs' – 'Mi'kmaq' is actually the correct spelling but over the years 'Micmac' has become the more commonly used name. These Indians still have much Gaelic vocabulary and musical traditions, such as 'mouth music', as a legacy of this. See also Alexander MacGillivray (20); John Ross (Cherokee) (39); William Drummond Stewart (41); and David Douglas (43), where empathetic associations with native Americans are highlighted.

LINE 30 'Old hallowed gold': The Holy Grail.

LINE 31 All except two ships returned to the Orkneys. Henry wintered in Nova Scotia, where he built a larger ship.

LINE 32 James Gunn – Chief of the Clan Gunn, whose clan is of Norse descent.

LINES 35 & 36 The Prospect Hill Memorial in Westford, Massachusetts is believed to be a testimony to this event, carved with either a crude outline of a tomahawk or a Knight's Templar carrying a shield, bearing the arms of Clan Gunn.

LINE 38 The Newport tower on Rhode Island.

LINE 40 Caithness became the place in the North where the Sinclair clan ruled.

(JARL) HENRY SINCLAIR

Saint-Clair! – The knights did name this Norman,
Who claimed his right to reign in Rosslyn.
His son did follow Royal Bruce
And clung to Norway's loyal truce.
Yet Shetland 'n Orkney, Jarl would hold   5
When their King's daughter's heart he stole,
And castles in those isles built he
As vassal in cold wild Wick's seas.
In Rosslyn where he dwelt, and Pentland,
From Robert, there he held his rent-land.   10
Whilst o'er in Norway, Eric's crowning
Much more, all ways lent empowering.
Wi' a fleet much bigger than the King's,
Achieve would Sinclair grander things.
From Bergen westwards they all filed   15
In zestful quest o' Faroe Isles,
Where heroes, Zeno joined Jarl's fleet
To steer those fellows on dark seas.
On Zeno's Map what then on followed,
In Venice, Carlo Zeno borrowed.   20
With twelve or thirteen ships through gales,
The west-bound winds did fill their sails.
On Newfoundland they found earth firstly,
But furious clans would oust them briskly.
Micmacs, that May in Nova Scotia   25
Did guard with care this noble Noah.
'Gooscap!' this sept did call Sinclair.
With Gaelic yet, their tongue compares.
Oak Island's Fort, raised in a hurry,
Old hallowed gold there he did bury.   30
Though turned so many hame on crafts,
James Gunn and Henry stayed on track
To sail at last to Massachusetts,
Where James Gunn died, and marked his new steps
On Prospect Hill's old man-of-arms,   35
Or auld imprints of Clan Gunn's badge.
The Newport spire Jarl next would build
On rude Rhode Island, then fulfilled
His fate as New World's founding father,
Sinclairs to view and vow as master.   40

2 JAMES GREGORY 1638–1675

Centuries of relentless persecution of the MacGregors, even to the point of proscribing their very name, produced partisans and geniuses of renown.

The family of Drumoak on Deeside took on the derivation Gregory. This family produced no less than 16 professors!

Apart from books on calculus and algebra's convergent series, James Gregory's greatest innovation was the 'Gregorian' reflecting telescope.

Gregory was also first to observe the splitting of light by a diffracting grating, as opposed to a prism, using seabirds' feathers for the grating. He also calculated ways of working out the distance from the Earth to the Sun.

Glossary/Explication

LINE 1 *'S Rioghal mo Dhream* (Gaelic), pronounced 'Sree-al mo gre-am', meaning 'Royal is my race' – the slogan of the MacGregors who, though descended from royalty, were continually outlawed unjustly, but retaliated with the sword.

LINE 2 *Clann Ghriogair* (Gaelic), pronounced 'Clown Greegair' – Clan Gregor, i.e. the MacGregors.

LINE 4 *Forrit* (Scots) – 'forward' i.e. they ran forward; they retaliated with their native military ardour.

LINE 5 On penalty of death on and off for almost three centuries, the MacGregors were forbidden from using their surname.

LINE 6 *Siller* (Scots) – 'silver'. With the feudal ethic of land over people (*duthchas*) taking a foothold in the Highlands, Clan Gregor's greedy ambitious neighbours profiteered from their misfortunes when they were continually hunted.

LINE 7 The famous Highland partisan Rob Roy MacGregor called himself 'Campbell', his mother's maiden name.

LINE 8 Their warlike deeds are eulogised in the heroic poetry of the Gaels.

LINE 9 This sept of this great clan in Deeside took the derivation 'Gregory', keeping part of their name and pride intact. Of the family of the minister John Gregory and Janet Anderson of Drumoak, James Gregory is the first in a long line of hereditary geniuses – 16 professors in all! – spanning three centuries of contributions to the human race in mathematics and science.

LINES 15–16 After learning much from his mother, James went to Italy to study, and then to St Andrews University. 'Goodly' is often used in Gaelic poetry (*deagh*) to extol the subject's virtues.

LINE 19 'Regius Chair' at St Andrews University.

LINE 20 He fell out with his fellow professors who found his 'New Philosophy' distasteful.

LINE 21 'Auld Reekie' is a colloquial name for Edinburgh.

LINES 29–34 Unfortunately he could not find a glassmaker able to produce the intricate lenses required. Newton and Gregory often worked concurrently on the same projects. It was to be a photo-finish between them both to produce the first mirror telescope, 'The Gregorian'. His second concave mirror reflected rays of light to the eye-piece. Interestingly, the word *gregor* in Ancient Greek means 'watchman', and the verb *gregoreo* means 'to watch'!

LINE 35 Using a seabird's feather creates schisms, i.e. the division or splitting between the feather's strands.

LINES 39–40 Adapted part of a nova-riddle for the mirror telescope.

JAMES GREGORY

'S Rioghal mo Dhream, declaims the slogan,
Clann Ghriogair's claim when ways were olden.
When feudal law replaced man's promise,
With two-edged sword, this race ran forrit.
The right to use their kingly name   5
Proscribed was too for siller gain.
Though aliases they did take on,
Their bravest vistas live in song.
A sept would stay by side o' Dee
Called Gregory by pride o' breed.   10
The claymore sheathed, replaced with quill,
Those Brainhearts, feats o' brain fulfilled.
Sixteen professors o' this clan
Did leave impressions over man.
This Gregory so goodly journeyed   15
To many places too to study,
Where through his trips his visions mirrored
Great Newton's Physics, which he'd further.
For Regius Chair, that sage betook,
But leave it there, in rage he would.   20
Auld Reekie's Mathematics Chair
Did steer he far with classic flair,
For Algebra's convergent series
And calculus on texts he'd leave us.
For truly James was his own man,   25
Who'd surely make for more advance
On telescopes that worked reflecting
But then his plot was non-effective,
For makers of yon glass to mould,
For James's cause were scant as gold.   30
A model type produce did Newton,
But blocking light this would for viewing.
But James did add a concave mirror,
Light rays to eye to copy inward.
Diffraction grating for light's schisms,   35
This rather claimed he than prime prisms.
He gauged the space from Earth to Sun,
As great a range his memoirs sum,
In a hall of mirrors viewing skies,
Beholding worlds for you to spy.   40

3 JOHN ARBUTHNOT 1667–1735

From Inverbervie in Aberdeenshire, John Arbuthnot studied at Marsichal College, Aberdeen, and then gained a medical degree from St Andrews University. He also translated Huygen's tract on probability and extended it by adding a few further games of chance. He wrote essays on natural history and mathematics, and became physician to Queen Anne, the last ruling Stewart monarch.

Arbuthnot claimed that the excess of male over female births was by divine providence. He is regarded as the originator of the application of probability to social statistics.

He was also famous for his witty satirical writings.

Glossary/Explication

LINES 1–4 The Union of the Crowns was in 1603 and the Union of the Parliaments was in 1707.

LINE 9 Queen Anne.

LINE 10 Although Anne was sister of the late wife of William of Orange, she was regarded contemptuously as 'The Queen of Cockneydom' by Highland Jacobites. There is a theory, however, that when on her deathbed, Anne changed her will and nominated the exiled James II as her successor – as opposed to Sophia, Electoress of Hanover – but her last wish was ignored.

LINES 13–16 The Battle of Killiecrankie in 1689 on behalf of the exiled King James II led to the Massacre of Glencoe in 1692, when many of the Clan Donald were murdered in their own beds by their guests, who were soldiers under the orders of King William's government, setting a precedent for an unethical colonial policy that would be used against native peoples in other places, especially in America, for example, the Massacre of Wounded Knee.

LINE 17 Huygen's tract on probability.

LINE 22 Saxon's nation, i.e. England. To Scots at that time, and even almost two centuries beyond, England was still very much a foreign country.

LINE 24 His best assertions – his essays.

LINE 25 Essay towards a natural history of the Earth.

LINE 26 Essay on the usefulness of mathematical learning.

LINE 27 He was elected a Fellow of the Royal Society in 1704.

LINE 29 He was appointed as physician to Queen Anne in 1705.

LINE 34 He claimed that the excess of male over female births was by divine providence.

LINES 37–38 With Alexander Pope, John Gray and Thomas Parnell he founded the Scriblerus Club in 1714, the purpose of which was to satirise bad poetry and pedantry.

JOHN ARBUTHNOT

From days of Union of the Crowns,
When heirs and rulers did go down,
Till governments appeared as one,
A hundred and four years had run.
But intervention cam' between   5
Frae Inverbervie, Aberdeen's
Great county, at that eastern side
Wi' stout a lad, wha'd be beside
The last Scot rightly on the throne –
For Jacobites, a thought to mourn.   10
He learned his skills and artful knowledge
Of medicine at Marischal College,
By which time clan and kith wid clash wi'
The English bands at Killiecrankie,
Then Glencoe ripe for raging ravage   15
And genocide, would bear the carnage.
But Huygen's Tract, at that same time,
And further chance in games besides,
This probability works named,
Guid John Arbuthnot did translate.   20
But after John's own graduation,
Was drafted he to Saxons' nation,
And mathematics share in sessions,
Whilst crafting at his great assertions
On annals of the Earth's past temper   25
And manuals for to ken maths better.
As Fellow too he was elected,
And settled too as top selected
And high physician to Queen Anne,
Then scientific work began   30
On birth of males own slight excess
Above females, highlight then stress,
As those statistics, social type,
Reports, all his, to quote 'divine!?'
As probability's application,   35
There called as first in any nation.
That witty lad sae kent in verses,
Satirically edged intensely.
When Jacobites, then took their chance,
On Anne's demise, did move to France.   40

4 ALEXANDER SELKIRK (1676–C.1721)

Born in Largo in Fife, Alexander Selkirk, a son of a cobbler, ran off to join English pirates sanctioned by the English government to prey upon an enemy country's merchant ships. They preyed off Spanish and Portuguese ships off the coast of South America.

After much plundering, the ship was so badly damaged that they put in at an island 400 miles east of Chile, where repairs would be carried out but the captain was in a hurry to set sail again. Selkirk demanded to be allowed to remain on the island and await rescue. His adventures became the story of Robinson Crusoe.

Glossary/Explication

LINES 9–13 The *Cinque Ports* was captained by William Dampier, an admired map maker but incompetent sea captain. Those English privateers were actually pirates sanctioned by their government to prey on their enemy's merchant ships. After three attempts to sail round Cape Horn in Southern Chile, the ship was so badly damaged and the crew so mutinous, that they put in at Mas a Tierra, an island 400 miles from the coast of Chile. Convinced of the ship's unseaworthiness, Selkirk demanded to be allowed to remain on the island and await rescue. At the outset, Selkirk packed some bedding, a firelock rifle, some powder, bullets, tobacco, a hatchet, a knife, a kettle, a Bible, his mathematical instruments, and some books. But he was to wait four years. The year was 1704.

LINE 23 Those escapees or defectors from the Spanish ships were closely clannish in that they spoke only their own language.

LINE 24 I have used 'rhetoric' here to represent both communication and therefore the inability to join in any lighthearted artistic expression or ceilidhing, highlighted in LINES 25 & 26 below.

LINES 25–26 He had already trained some of the island's goats when they were kids. After being rescued, he told of tales of dancing and singing with his pets in the moonlight.

LINE 34 He kept a fire burning on a nearby hill, hoping to lure in a passing English ship.

LINE 35 In early 1709, Selkirk saw sails on the horizon. Recognising the English flag, he ran to meet the long boats. Woode Rogers captained the English privateer 'Duke'. Interestingly enough, the pilot of the ship was none other than William Dampier, former captain of the *Cinque Ports*. They were startled by this 'wildman' running at them along the beach. Selkirk was finally rescued but had not spoken for so long that he had forgotten some vocabulary.

LINE 36 Selkirk's outstanding seamanship helped Rodgers capture a richly loaded Spanish merchant ship. Rodgers made Selkirk captain over the ship for the voyage back to England.

LINES 37–38 On his return journey, he met the essayist Richard Steele who recorded Selkirk's adventures for a publication called *The Englishman*.

LINES 39–40 Years later, Daniel Defoe, the English spy and author, would use Selkirk's story as the inspiration for the novel *Robinsoe Crusoe*.

ALEXANDER SELKIRK

Yon package holidays these days
Do have us spoiled in varied ways.
Except your money, fare and bags,
You're left no worries there and back.
Health-life insurance don't forget,   5
Lest by imprudence you're all left
And landed where most lack your language
Well stranded in those lands to languish.
Envisage, though, in distant times,
And in an olden different clime,   10
And being encircled by strewn acres
Of heaving billows' high blue breakers.
This island paradise that's tiny
Does highlight far a life that's mighty.
Abounding fresh are pools for paddling,   15
And fountain heads are cool for calming,
But rats are gnawing on your feet!
And cats by scores filch from you, sleep.
A hut built of pimento wood
Does shut ills out like shelters should.   20
Your clothes designs are ever from
Cured goat-skin lined on every wall.
Defectors ship-wrecked, closely clannish,
For rhetoric ken only Spanish,
While goats and cats as moonlight friends   25
You host and dance and groom as guests
Durations' span, you have no say.
You're famous as a castaway!
Your cruise-ship took you round the Horn,
But lose it, you did out in storms.   30
As Sandy Selkirk, life you started,
Frae Largo in East Fife you parted
You eat fruit, plants, goat meat, with milk,
And keep your fire, on heat up hill.
When that ship comes to cruise you homewards   35
With Spanish plunder, through the oceans,
To Richard Steele, you tell your tales.
With privateers you set your sails.
He cons Defoe who fakes this further,
And calls Crusoe! his gainful plunder.   40

5 JAMES FRANCIS EDWARD KEITH 1696–1758

From Peterhead, this son of the Earl of Marischal was a staunch Jacobite.

Under the banner of the Earl of Mar, he was a principal leader of the Jacobite uprising in 1715, the failure of which led to him to flee.

The Empress Anne of Russia made him Governor of the Ukraine. He spurned the affections of her successor, and fled to Prussia to become Field-Marshal to Frederick the Great. He won many battles in the Seven Years War. He died from his wounds at the Battle of Hochkirk.

Statues commemorate him in Peterhead and Berlin.

Glossary/Explication

LINES 1–4 True Thomas, also known as Thomas the Rhymer, was a poet and seer who lived in the days of Wallace, who proclaimed that 'A day would come when a great battle north of the Clyde would take place that the language and culture of the Gael would be as it once was.' 'The Song of the Highland Clans' was composed in 1715 to incite all the nobles of Scotland, Highland and Lowland, to stand together and restore Scotland to its most ancient independence, under the banner of the exiled Stewarts. Its first line declares 'This is the time when the prophecy will be fulfilled for us.' The Jacobite rising of 1715, that culminated in the Battle of Sherrifmuir near Dunblane on 13 November of that year, did not succeed because of the ineffective leadership of Mar.

LINE 6 *Dags* is a Gaelic word for the old Highland metal pistols made in Doune, Perthshire.

LINE 7 'Bobbin John' was John Erskine, Earl of Mar.

LINE 8 Several songs about the '15 have been written mentioning Bobbin John.

LINE 9 From the song 'Sherrifmuir', by Robert Burns. 'I saw the battle sair an teuch'. *Teuch* (Scots), pronounced 'tyooch', means 'sore and tough'.

LINES 11–14 'Al-u-ba' – 'Alba', the Gaelic word for 'Scotland'. I have spelled it this way as an approximate guide to its pronunciation.

LINES 15–16 'The Day Oor King Comes o'er the Water' – 'Lady Keith's Lament', a most haunting Jacobite song.

LINE 26 James, being deeply in love with another, did not want to be Elizabeth's lover, and therefore made his escape to Prussia.

LINE 27 Frederick the Great was the famous Emperor of Prussia.

LINES 37–40 William I of Prussia presented a statue of Keith to his home town and erected one in Berlin.

JAMES FRANCIS EDWARD KEITH

Yes! Yon True Thomas saw a day
That was to come back for the Gael
When strife north o' the Clyde would ravage
Their rights, for ever might be salvaged.
For gallant clansmen clad in tartan,   5
Well armed with targes, dags and daggers
Would race to Bobbin John's brave banner,
Whose name in song would long raise ardour.
'I saw the battle, sair an teugh',
Did ca' oor Rabbie swearing truth.   10
Since Al-u-ba did bow bereaving,
Its parliament with crown yet grieving,
Would little match wi' yon famed fate,
Of bringing back the sovereign state.
'The day oor King comes o'er the water',   15
A dame would sing, but war would cost her,
For fealty's face her man resembled,
Who'd bravely bear well armed, assembled.
When Sherrifmuir was o'er and gone,
With servitude he roamed abroad   20
To Moscow, where he soon would gain,
An offer there, to rule Ukraine,
As sponsored by the Empress Anne,
Who on her dying breath next marked,
Him for the Empress next in line,   25
Which cause did ever vex his mind.
So to Frederick the Great then fleeing,
In whose terrific reign then steering
His army, which he led like lightning,
So manly risked himself while fighting.   30
In that hard seven year long struggle,
This marshal served in tearful troubles,
Till Hochkirk's Field o' dark hue, hellish,
This northern chief alas would perish.
This trusty blade they'd ne'er forget.   35
In Prussia's state, James yet is kent.
For features next did build their king,
In Peterhead and in Berlin
For values of the old ways past,
In statues for this bold Brainheart.   40

6 SIR HUGH DALRYMPLE 1700–1753

Sir Hugh (or possibly Hew) Dalrymple, Lord Drummore, invented drainage systems primarily for the sake of reclaiming bog land for the use of agriculture, leading to the development of the gutter drainage system that every house now has.

He was believed to be the brother of the Earl of Stair, whose infamous name is tarred as being the mastermind of the Massacre of Glencoe in 1792 and the Union of the Parliaments in 1707.

Glossary/Explication

LINE 11 Lord Drummore – Sir Hugh Dalrymple.

LINE 35 A drone, i.e. the drone of a bagpipe.

LINES 38–40 A branch of this family was the Earl of Stair, infamous for the Union of Parliaments and the Massacre of Glencoe.

SIR HUGH DALRYMPLE

How often times in fields sae rotten,
In soggy slime wi' heels sae sodden,
Wi' marshy squelch! to pull releasing
Did harshly wrench you, your feet greetin',
To find that, as you eased both down   5
Beside a shallow piece of ground,
Which innocent, aye it appears
Would drink you in, and bring back tears?
Your purpose there might well slow down,
Where much these quagmires do abound.   10
Lord Drummore asked once in this vein,
How such coarse land might be reclaimed:
'Diverting floods, I do believe,
By bending, turning routes, we'll need
To place first sunken pipes beneath,   15
To make this surplus mire retreat.
Through perforations punched by piercing
Strewn there serrated, sucking, streaming
In pipes joined up from bog to brook,
We might those furrowed swamps re-route.   20
To daily drain the fields by hand
Could scarcely claim nor clear the land.'
His innovation did much drying,
Like irrigation, without trying.
For wilderness which knew no function,   25
Was tilled well into pure production,
With crops to yield on farms sae muckle
In broader fields of agriculture.
Which principle, it needs no telling,
Could visibly far keep your dwelling   30
From flooding badly through its roof,
By running channels, hewn in two
To join the drain-rone, to the corner,
As border vein, for losing water
Through gutters which sing like a drone   35
To flutter with the finest tone.
This system all which looks sae simple
Was first installed by Hugh Dalrymple,
Whose name must surely better fare,
Than sare Kirkcudbright's Earl o' Stair.   40

7 ALEXANDER CRUDEN 1699–1770

Born in Aberdeen, Alexander Cruden, son of a merchant and bailey,
received an MA from Marischal College. He was later employed in
London as a corrector for the press. Also a bookseller of renown,
he was appointed bookseller to the Queen.

He commenced work on his Concordance to the Bible, eventually
dedicating it to Queen Caroline, the consort to George II, who
promised to remember him, but she died suddenly a few days later.

Eventually he was rewarded by George III for his second edition.
He also published a Bible dictionary.

He was known as Alexander the Corrector.

Glossary/Explication

LINE 1 James VI published an Authorised version of the Bible in 1611, standardising the text, called the King James Bible.

LINE 2 To the credit of James VI's administration, ordinary people could read the Bible themselves to see what it really said, without the approval or overseeing of church hierarchy – a revolutionary liberty for its time.

LINE 4 Timothy II, Chapter 2, verse 15 of that Bible says: 'Study to shew thyself approved unto God, a workman that needeth not be ashamed, rightly dividing the word of truth.'

LINE 5 *Aiberdeen*: Aberdeen (Scots).

LINE 7 'His papers' – his MA.

LINES 9–12 The Old Testament was first written in Hebrew and the New Testament was first written in Greek.

LINES 13–16 The purpose of the *Concordance to the Holy Bible*. See note on LINE 30 below. His work is still in print.

LINE 17 Queen Caroline, the consort of George II.

LINES 18–21 Caroline graciously promised to remember him but, unfortunately for him, she died suddenly.

LINES 22–24 With the expense of publishing his Concordance and the neglect of his business, he sank into melancholy despondency, of which he had a history, and entered the private asylum of Bethnal Green for nine weeks and six days.

LINES 25–28 Being a kindly, harmless man, he took in a poor lady from the streets, and instructed her in her duties, and she remained in his service until his death.

LINE 30 A Concordance is an alphabetical arrangement of words with citations of passages concerned with word derivations, in order that the student of the Bible has an aid or tool, to research for his or her own self, comparing the usages of one word in particular in its various usages and in various contexts, in order to gain a greater or more in depth understanding of what is written.

LINES 35 He received a hero's welcome on his return home to Aberdeen, where he stayed for one year, before returning to London.

LINE 37 'Closet' – a biblical term meaning 'a solitary place of prayer'.

LINE 40 His appellation.

ALEXANDER CRUDEN

The King James Bible laid the base,
And in great triumph paved the way
With right for folks to have God's truth
In sight of him, to stand approved.
Frae Aiberdeen came Alex Cruden,   5
Wha's ever keen eye as a student
To London brought him with his papers,
Where further work would win him favours.
For search did Alex Hebrew words,
And testaments of Greek too worked,   10
With no church cleric's hands at all,
To those words therein catalogued.
From texts, would each word be collated,
Indexed to read where these related,
To greater contexts from the verses,   15
Relating all sense-forming tenses.
To first Queen Consort, as book-agent,
His finished work was passed for wages.
Him 'have in mind,' said she, she'd surely,
But Caroline's sad decease duly   20
Then left no money in that bank,
So to melancholy, this man sank.
In Bethnal Green, for the insane
Interned they he, for his own sake.
Yet on release he showed compassion   25
There on the streets in homely fashion
To a poorly girl, who entered, stayed,
And stood with him to spend her days.
But King George sponsored Issue Two
Of his *Concordance*, which accrued   30
Much well o'er-due outstanding balance,
As revenue for Alexander.
His dictionary of the Scriptures
Would link or marry word wi' picture,
Though sae revered, for yin hale year,   35
In Aiberdeen tae win great cheer.
In London's closet of his there,
In godly posture, locked in prayer,
Alas dead! found they, him known better
As Alexander the Corrector.   40

8 ROBERT SMITH 1722–1777

Robert Smith was the son of a baker from Loughton, near Dalkeith, where he qualified as a journeyman carpenter, then emigrated to Philadelphia.

He was greatly influential in the upgrading of pricing, payment, design and maintenance standards in American industry. He designed and built many buildings there that are now of great architectural and historical importance.

When war with Great Britain seemed likely, Smith employed his skills in the service of the patriots. He died whilst working on the barracks for the Continental Army at Billingsport.

He is regarded as being America's first architect.

Glossary/Explication

LINES 1–5 It is thought that skyscrapers were first built in the Old Town of Edinburgh.

LINE 6 *Mair* – more (Scots).

LINE 8 Robert Smith was descended from a family of masons, carpenters and master builders. One of his ancestors was James Smith (1645–1731), a leading Scottish architect and surveyor for the Royal Works in Scotland, until succeeded by William Adam, father of architects Robert and James Adam, who seem to have given Robert Smith his first job.

LINES 11–12 It is believed that Smith began his architectural training in the early 1740s, as a newly qualified journeyman carpenter working for William Adam at Dalkeith Park, on the estate of the Duke of Buccleuch.

LINE 13 Shortly after Adam's death, Smith appeared in Philadelphia.

LINE 14 Gunning and Bedford was the company who gave him his first known commission in America.

LINES 15–16 The construction of the second Presbyterian Church began in 1749 on Third and Arch Streets.

LINES 17–20 Smith professionalised the influential Carpenters' Company of Philadelphia. Following the model of the Worshipful Company of Carpenters, the Carpenters' Company was formed to set up uniform standards of pricing and payments, to maintain high level design and workmanship in building practices. All those who belonged to the group had the opportunity to study models and treatises in the Company's library.

LINES 21–22 Several of Smith's books went into the Company's library upon his death.

LINES 23–28 Some famous buildings Smith designed. Mount Pleasant at Fairmount Park was designed for Captain John Macpherson. Princeton College – See John Witherspoon (9).

LINE 29 George III had imposed such burdensome taxation on Americans that they, with the help of some Scots, decided to break away. See also John Witherspoon (9) and John Paul Jones (14).

LINE 30 The Patriots – supporters of American independence. Hence 'Rebel Robbie'.

LINES 31–34 He designed military architecture to protect Philadelphia from British attack, including an elaborate system of underwater fortifications in the Delaware River that stymied British communications off the coast. He was working on a group of barracks for the Continental Army at Billingsport, New Jersey, whilst under attack, at the time of his death. *Burling* – sometimes spelled 'birling', means 'whorling' or 'churning' (Scots).

LINE 37 The Friends' Meeting Building Ground.

LINE 40 His appellation.

ROBERT SMITH

They say Manhattan's great tall breezy
Spires claimed a pattern frae Auld Reekie.
Their size, their shape, their height or girth,
Disguises place and time of birth.
But if skyscrapers o'er seas travelled,   5
There's insight mair that's no mean marvel.
Fine monoliths o' grand visage,
Well honoured with the artist's craft,
Did hail down from a baker's boy
Who frae wee Loughton stayed employed   10
At Dalkeith Park, with William Adam,
As master-craftsman, till this talents
To Philadelphia, brought him over,
Where Gunning-Bedford sought this rover.
To that wee church indeed give birth,   15
Where Arch Street's junction meets the Third
A bright alliance he there did form,
To price and standards be conformed
Uphold and lift high key design
Of workmanship, aye he'd delight.   20
'Twas for this intent, time he took
Recording his designs in books:
That gem, St Peter's, Franklin's House,
Macpherson's, nearer at Fairmount,
That worthy school too, Princeton College   25
Where Witherspoon would bring much knowledge.
There with no hesitance nor doubt
Raised Smith the President's own house,
Then faced with loss from German Geordie,
With patriots, joined Rebel Robbie,   30
Next set to raise forts underwater,
In Delaware's old burling bottom.
With willing soul, real skill in barrage,
In Billingsport, he built his barracks.
'Twas under this sheer strain Smith died,   35
And buried is he there inside
The building ground, where friends a' meet,
Which still is found where ends Arch Street,
Where true friends paid this man respect,
As USA's first architect.   40

9 JOHN WITHERSPOON 1723–1794

Descending from John Knox, and born and raised in Yester Parish near Edinburgh, John Witherspoon went to public school in Haddington, then received an MA from the University of Edinburgh.

He became minister of Beith, then a prisoner of Jacobites, then minister of Paisley.

He was invited to America to become President of New Jersey's College, where he made great alterations. His distinguished abilities pointed him out as one of the most proper delegates to the convention which formed the Republican Constitution.

He was elected to the General Congress and signed the American Declaration of Independence, which was modelled on the Scots' Declaration of Arbroath of 1320.

Glossary/Explication

LINE 1 Yester Parish is just south of Edinburgh.

LINES 3–6 John Knox, the founder of the Scottish Reformation.

LINE 8 *Thirled* – tethered (Scots). Calvin was John Knox's mentor.

LINES 9–12 Both John and his father had attended public school at Haddington, acquiring a high reputation for soundness of judgement and clearness of mind.

LINE 13 'Auld Reekie' – a nickname for Edinburgh. At the age of 14, Witherspoon attended Edinburgh University and distinguished himself for diligence and rapid literary attainments, an uncommon taste in sacred criticism, and unusual precision of thought.

LINE 14 Beith, Ayrshire – his next church.

LINES 15–18 Charlie, i.e. Bonnie Prince Charlie. The Battle of Falkirk was fought on 17 January 1746, which the Jacobites won. As spectators, Witherspoon, amongst others, was caught and taken prisoner in Doune Castle in Perthshire for a time, before escaping.

LINES 19–22 Paisley minister until emigrating to America, to take charge as president of Princeton College of New Jersey in August 1768. See also Robert Smith (8).

LINES 23–24 *Guid* – good (Scots). *Afore* – before (Scots). He introduced all the most liberal and modern improvements of Europe into philosophy, embracing public law.

LINES 25–30 He founded a course of history in the college, emphasising principles of taste and the rules of writing in his manner. He possessed an admirable faculty for governing and exciting emulation among committed pupils, many of whom graduated to become distinguished for eminent services to their country as divines, legislators and patriots.

LINE 31–38 He espoused the cause of the Americans against the English ministry, and helped to found the Constitution. At this respectable assembly, his wisdom astounded the professors of law. In early 1776, he was elected as representative to the General Congress by the people of New Jersey, assisting deliberations on the question of a declaration of independence. When asked if the country was ripe for this move, his witty answer was 'Not only ripe but rotting'.

LINE 39 4 July – American Independence Day.

LINE 40 The Declaration of Arbroath 1320 – 'So long as but one hundred of us lives, we will not yield to the domination of the English.'

JOHN WITHERSPOON

In Yester years, and from that parish,
This blessed revered man called and carried
As rowdily would his antecedent,
The powerful views he'd aye be breathin',
As call on high, frae wee soap-box,   5
Like Scotland's fiery, feared John Knox.
John Witherspoon, who had this schooling,
Was thirled too, to Calvin's ruling,
For father's footsteps trudged he too,
In Haddington's then public school.   10
In judgement quick and sound, with vision,
Incumbent with astounding wisdom,
Which blossomed in Auld Reekie, reaching
His followers of Beith, wi' preaching.
When Charlie's men at Falkirk fought,   15
Bystanders then with John, were caught
And placed in holds o' Castle Doune,
Escaping boldly by full moon.
A Paisley pulpit next he'd spurn,
Embrace the New World, then become   20
Professor of and the elect
New Jersey's College President.
Aye John's guid name had gone afore him,
And long did raise glad songs, adoring,
Distinguished truly in these spheres,   25
Which willing students did revere,
Of patriots and dignitaries,
So greatly sought was him sae worthy
As generation-building man,
Who'd helm that nation with his hand.   30
With English Ministry resisting,
Its fickle tyranny desisting,
This true free son did swear his pledge on
The New Republic's brave Convention.
When sought to know if time was dawning,   35
Said John 'Not only ripe but rotting!'.
Elected, by all represented,
To General Congress accepted,
Assured was John that July Fourth,
As Bruce once was, in oor Arbroath.   40

10 ADAM SMITH 1723–1790

*Adam Smith, from Kirkcaldy, regarded as the father of free enter-
prise, was to take his place at the head of the first school of
economics, one that continues and is known as a 'classical school'
to this day.*

*Although he originally studied at Oxford, he went to France,
which held a special attraction for Scottish people because of the
'Auld Alliance'. There he met Voltaire, and started to write his
masterpiece,* The Wealth of Nations, *which is still regarded as the
foundational treatise of our modern economy.*

He is regarded as the very first political economist in the world.

Glossary/Explication

LINES 1–4 In 1751/52, aged 28, as Professor of Logic at Glasgow University, Smith took
the Chair of Moral Philosophy. In 1759 he published his *Theory of Moral Sentiments*,
revising it until his death. Smith wrote his 'economics' as a philosopher. Philosophy then
included a study of jurisprudence (the science of the philosophy of human law). A study
of justice leads to a study of legal systems, which leads to the study of government,
which leads to the study of political economy.

LINE 2 *Steer* – stir (Scots).

LINE 5 'A profound knowledge of the real occupations of mankind', exhibited in *The
Wealth of Nations*.

LINE 6 'Roles', i.e. the roles of people in society.

LINES 9–8 From his own words, '...it is not his aim to espouse the interests of any class.
He is concerned with promoting the wealth of the entire nation. And wealth consists of
the goods, which all the people of society consume – a democratic and radical philos-
ophy of wealth. Gone is the notion of gold, treasures, kingly hoards... prerogatives of
merchants or farmers or working guilds. We are in the modern world where the flow
of goods and services consumed by everyone constitutes the ultimate aim and end of
economic life. Every individual is continually exerting himself to find out the most
advantageous employment for whatever capital he can command. It is his own advan-
tage, indeed, and not that of society, which he has in view. But the study of his own
advantage naturally, or rather necessarily, leads him to prefer that employment which
is most advantageous to the society. He generally, indeed, neither intends to promote
the public interest, nor knows how much he is promoting it. By preferring the support
of domestic to that of foreign industry, he intends only his security; and by directing
that industry in such a manner as its produce may be of the greatest value, he intends
only his own gain, and he is in this, as in many other cases, led by an invisible hand to
promote an end which was no part of his intention.'
Nae mettur what will aye persist on – No matter what will always exist (Scots).

LINES 39–40 Kirkcaldy was his home town. The world's first political economist is his
appellation.

ADAM SMITH

The *Theory of Moral Sentiments*,
Did steer the hornet's nervous nest,
With budget oft times to include in
The studies of life's jurisprudence.
One man's appealing profound knowledge   5
Would far reveal in roles from yon age,
For Adam Smith, his best foundation,
To grant his gift – his *Wealth of Nations*.
Not dealing through class forms thereby,
Nor seeking who had what nor why,   10
It ne'er embraced concerns of class,
But entire nations' wealth en masse.
'And wealth,' he said, 'consists of goods,
Themselves, the nations will consume
On Wealth for All, my core opinions,   15
Will rest or fall, in most dominions.
With notion gone of precious treasures,
Aye hoards o' lords, and merchants' measures.
Where there in new world's flow of goods
And service fulfilled does conclude   20
The utter end of mortals' strife,
And sum of economic life.
Those self same persons well exerting
For welfare ends of self, invest with
The cash to deal from their own hands,   25
For that good yield, some may command.
They hardly intend to promote
The masses' interests too nor know,
Promoting, how much one does it,
Foreknowing with such conscious wit.   30
One's domain's inner ways preferring,
To foreign industry depending,
And is that much directed from it,
To give as such fine merit for it.
Though animals can live like islands,   35
On man it falls to inter-bargain.
Self-regulating market's system,
Nae mettur what will aye persist on.'
Quo': Kirkcaldy's own World's First
Political Economist.   40

11 JOHN BROADWOOD 1732–1812

Taking up the trade of his father as a carpenter, John Broadwood, with written recommendation from his local laird, went to London as an apprentice to a Swiss harpsichord maker.

He learned the craft very quickly, married the harpsichord maker's daughter, went into partnership in the business and took over its running.

Together with another Scotsman, they worked on what became known as the 'English Grand Action'.

He took out the first patent of the 'piano and forte pedals' and eventually developed the Grand Piano. Some of his first clients included top composers such as Mozart, Chopin, Beethoven and Lizst.

Glossary/Explication

LINES 1–14 'Cockburnspath', pronounced 'Co-burnspath'. John Broadwood went to London to work for Burkat Shudi, a Swiss harpsichord maker.

LINES 17–19 The enthusiastic apprentice soon not only gained Shudi's daughter's hand in marriage, but a partnership in the firm, which was renamed accordingly. In 1771, the running of the business was handed over completely to John.

LINES 21–28 Together with his assistant, another Scotsman called Robert Stoddart, they worked on what was then called the English Grand Action, patented in 1777 in Stoddart's name. Meanwhile, John was improving and modifying the square piano. He took out the first patent for the 'piano and forte pedals', replacing the knee and hand levers on existing models.

LINE 27 *Auld* – old (Scots).

LINE 28 *Guid* – good (Scots).

LINES 29–32 Description of the Grand Piano. By adding a separate brass ridge to improve the quality of tone of the notes, he also extended its range by introducing the six octave grand.

LINE 35 He also developed techniques for mass producing pianos, so much so that by the mid-1790s, the firm gave up the manufacturing of harpsichords completely, as a result of the success of the grand piano.

JOHN BROADWOOD

East Lothian's auld Cockburnspath
Need boast of him wha's noble craft,
Who'd harvest therein, true new skills
As carpenter which would fulfil
With gathered silver up for flitting,   5
His chance to live in London City.
Aged nearly thirty, did John go,
With cheer and merriment of soul,
To that metropolis sae sassy
Of grandest operas sae classy,   10
Where Burkat Shudi ran his shop,
Festooned a' through with harpsichords,
Which his fair hands, designed for making
In Switzerland, refined for playing.
So at the firm was he apprenticed   15
In partnership to be accepted
In business, as a bright free flame,
Whilst Shudi's lass as bride he gained.
With quick wit, John's tuned hand next turned
On business jobs to man, then run.   20
A fellow Scot whose name was Stoddart,
Then helped with John, to make yon product
Known as the English Grand's full size,
From start, to finish, and arise.
But John's real forte pedals' patent   25
Would long be more preferred, than dated
Auld awkward hand and knee-worked levers,
For what guid grand plan he would leave us.
A brass ridge put on, segregated,
And classic true tone there related,   30
Extended to six octave grand,
Which let his new gift always have
A name with Chopin, Liszt, Beethoven,
Of fame, which John is still yet known in
Of grand pianos o' renown,   35
Enhancing class o' core-deep sound,
Whose ever soothing sonic tone
Is heard in music hall, in home,
In orchestra on stage or stand,
In concert, mass-ball great and grand.   40

12 ALEXANDER (SECUNDUS) MONRO
1733–1817

Alexander Monro, Professor of Anatomy and Surgery at the University of Edinburgh, was a member of a family of anatomists spanning 126 years – he was preceded in his post by his father and succeeded by his son. They were all named Alexander.

Monro is notable for the 10,000 or so medical records that he kept detailed in 33 volumes, and for his discovery of the Foramen of Monro, which links the lateral and the third ventricles of the brain.

I have opened this piece alluding back to his ancestors, the mountaineers for the Earls of Ross, and the more remote Irish Milesian Princes.

Glossary/Explication

LINES 1–2 Dungivern on the River Roe, County Derry. The seat of the O'Cahans, from whom the Monros, or Munros, sprang. They are known patronymically as the seed of O'Cahan or, in Gaelic, *Siol Ui Chathain,* pronounced 'shee-awl oo cha-ain'.

LINES 3–4 Descended from the lawful son of *Domhnall Ui Chathain*, Prince of Fermana, who came to Alba (Scotland) with his sister, who married Angus MacDonald of Islay, the head of Clan Donald, also known as the Lord of the Isles. *Albain* is a Gaelic derivation for 'Scotland'.

LINE 6 The Monros accepted feudal charters from the Earls of Ross. Donald O'Cahan is their ancestor, from whom the place *Fearann Domhnaill* is named. They proved their worth as fit mountaineers by providing for their feudal superiors 'a pair of white gloves, or three pennies and a ball of snow in mid-summer', which the hollows of his mountain patrimony could provide at all times of the year. The Monros, with honour, retained hold of the lands.

LINE 7 Several Monros were involved in the American independence movement. Coincidentally, the eagle, apart from being their clan's symbol, is also the emblem of the USA.

LINE 10 'Heart o' – a classical expression, meaning 'the deepest inner part of'.

LINES 11–15 In 1754, he was appointed as conjoint Professor of Anatomy and Surgery at Edinburgh, along with his father.

LINE 15 'Chair' – Chair of Anatomy, Edinburgh University.

LINES 17–30 Monro is notable for all those medical records in 33 volumes, and for his discovery of the Foramen of Monro, explained in his publication *Observations on the Structure and Functions of the Nervous System.* 'His guide' – his book.

LINES 32–34 'Guid laddy' – his own son, who succeeded him in Anatomy and Surgery, and lectured, amongst other things, on the phrenology of the serial killer Burke (of Burke and Hare fame), whilst dissecting him. *Sare* – sore (Scots).

LINES 35–36 This is recorded in one of his publications, called *The Structure and Physiology of Fishes Explained and Compared With Those of Man and Other Animals.*

LINES 37–40 The three consecutive Alexander Monros were Primus, Secundus and Tertius. All three held Professorship of Anatomy, spanning an entire period of 126 years.

ALEXANDER (SECUNDUS) MONRO

Yon eerie Castle on the Roe,
Though *Siol Ui Chathain*, called their own.
By intermarriage through Clan Donald,
Came into Alba true to follow,
And ground there leased in yon far north,   5
As mountaineers fit for Clan Ross.
Their badge does show the mighty eagle,
As Clan Monro, so rightly regal.
A great man weel kent by yon name
As Brainheart, researched heart o' brain   10
While really apt at mathematics
To gear his hand to scalpel practice
Anatomy next in pursuit
At fast a pace, to fill the shoes
O' his guid faither, in the Chair,   15
Of which his labours wid compare,
For true to reckon these was Sandy,
As proved through records he'd haud handy,
Ten thousand of which keep did he,
Set down in volumes, thirty three.   20
The Foramen of Monro's debut
Then bore a very honoured breakthrough.
The lateral with third this links
Grey cavities which sit within
Connecting this inside the brain's   25
Own centre, which his guide explained
In commentaries well expanded,
And documented, understanding
Of his perceptions in the structures
All with the nervous system's functions.   30
Although his father held the sway,
His own guid laddie next would lay
Hands on phrenology's sare work,
And quarter skull of killer Burke,
Then physiology of fishes,   35
To mirror also with folk's tissues.
Of first and second names three times,
From birth to death yon Chair defined,
One hundred years and twenty six
Of studies deemed a clever mix.   40

13 JAMES WATT 1736–1819

James Watt was born in Greenock and brought up in poverty and sadness. Although his apprenticeship as an instrument maker was incomplete, he was eventually appointed in this profession to Glasgow University. There he learnt about latent heat from the Scottish scientist, Joseph Black. He fixed the university's model of a Newcomen engine and developed it by adding a separate condenser, a chamber into which the steam would be kept cool, whilst the first chamber was kept hot, thus inventing steam power.

In this piece is a list of his major steam-powered innovations and others, in the form of an equation.

Glossary/Explication

LINE 5 'Greenhorn' – novice, newcomer. He knew no riches.

LINE 9 *Sarely* – sorely (Scots). His incomplete apprenticeship as an instrument maker caused him to be disadvantaged on each new interview.

LINES 11–16 He managed to gain employment with Glasgow University. When the University's Newcomen engine broke down, James came up with the idea of producing a separate chamber, or condenser, into which the steam would enter and remain cool, whilst the first chamber remained hot. The two functions would therefore cancel each other out. *Sook* – suck (Scots).

LINES 17–18 The steam-powered industrial revolution. Eventually Watt went into partnership with Bolton, a successful businessman from Birmingham, where they made and sold steam engines. See also William Murdoch (18).

LINE 19 Central heating became a by-product of his invention, as it created a way for steam to be sent up through pipes in buildings.

LINE 20 He and his assistant, William Murdoch (18), added mechanical accessories to his engine that altered the linear movement of a piston into a wheel-like circular motion. This alteration permitted manufacturers to operate machinery in more space-, time- and cost-effective ways.

LINES 21–22 The Centrifugal Governor was the first of a breed of devices which could control an engine's speed automatically.

LINES 23–26 Horse power (HP) was his concept as a marketing device for his fire engines to illustrate to those concerned the force of his engine against that of a horse.

LINE 29 Rhyming synonym for the gasometer.

LINE 30 He suggested the screw propeller half a century before it was first employed.

LINES 31–32 The letter copier, patented in 1780. He formed a company to produce his copier, which was highly successful.

LINES 33–34 The term horse power (HP) (see notes on LINES 23–26 above) was Watt's innovation. 'Watt' posthumously replaced 'HP' as the term for a standard unit of power.

LINE 34 *Hames* – homes (Scots).

LINES 35–38 Massive employment. See note on LINES 17–18 above.

LINE 39 *Ain* – own (Scots)

JAMES WATT

For all debating kind who'd ask,
This long equation might you grasp?
If you kent how was raised this Scot,
Would you tell now of ways of want?
A greenhorn to that silver spoon,   5
This Greenock poor lad, gripped with gloom,
Four brothers lost did in his youth,
Old mother, with his sisters too.
Though rebuffed sarely each new chance,
Fine instruments still he could craft,   10
Wi' clever thoughts in how things clicked,
An engine's water-pump he'd fix
To sook the steam, another chamber,
Would cool and keep the stuff much safer.
Whilst first the other stayed yet hot,   15
For this, this one, the patent got.
Which roused that century's solution
Of power rendered revolution.
Plus vigorous heat's circulation,
Plus pistons with wheel in rotation,   20
Plus governor that's centrifugal's,
Own up or lower, revs would choose all.
Plus proved horse power, a gauge, high, mighty,
To boost yon towering sare fire-fighting,
For red fire engine for concern o'   25
The entire ending of inferno.
Plus his slide rule for calculation,
And guid guide too for graduation.
Plus his gauge-gas-use trued clock teller,
Plus first great scrambling screw propeller,   30
Plus must to quicken office needs,
A drudge to print and copy sheets.
Plus thrust in units of his name,
Sae current too in all our hames.
Plus more work for two million folk   35
Before e'er one could lift the dole
Of industry's own changing mode.
So big did play the same, a role.
This famed Scot o' his ain wee nation,
Is James Watt o' this same equation.   40

14 JOHN PAUL JONES 1747–1792

Born in the Stewardry of Kirkcudbright, John Paul, son of a gardener, entered the British Merchant Navy as a boy. He received his first command in 1773 but he killed a mutinous crewman and fled to North America, where he added Jones to his name and obtained a lieutenant's commission in the Continental Navy.

His adventures here outline his major martial achievements which caused him to reach the rank of Commodore.

Through intrigue, he became Rear Admiral in the Russian Navy. For the same reason he left there for France, where he died. His body was eventually re-interred in the USA.

Glossary/Explication

LINES 1–6 The name 'Stewart' or 'Stuart' is derived from 'Steward'. Kirkcudbright was never known as a 'shire' but as a 'stewardry'. I've drawn here on the comparison of Adam in the Bible, and that of his own father's occupation, i.e. a gardener, comparing it etymologically with the term 'stewardry'.

LINES 7–8 Post-Culloden and the end of the Stewart dynasty.

LINES 13–16 In 1773, he took command of a merchant vessel in the West Indies but killed a mutinous crewman, then fled to North America where he concealed his identity by adding the surname 'Jones'.

LINES 17–18 George III imposed such burdensome taxation on Americans that they, with the help of some Scots, broke away. See also John Witherspoon (9) and Robert Smith (8).

LINE 19 'One of those' – in this case, America.

LINE 20 At the outbreak of war with Britain in 1775, John Paul Jones went to Philadelphia, and obtained a lieutenant's commission in the Continental Navy.

LINES 21–22 In 1776, he was captain of the sloop *Providence*.

LINES 25–30 In 1777 he commanded the sloop *Ranger*, sailed to France and received from the French the first salute given to the new American flag by them, after which he terrorised the coastal population of Britain. 'Birlinn' is used here to mean 'swift ship', hence 'fleet fleet'. As commodore, he commanded a mixed fleet of French and Americans, capturing 17 merchantmen and six Royal Naval ships.

LINES 31–32 A famous quotation of his in defiance of the British during a sea battle.

LINES 34–40 Although hailed as a hero in both Paris and Philadelphia, Jones encountered political rivalry and never again held a major American command at sea. In 1788 Catherine II (The Great) appointed him Rear Admiral of the Russian Navy. But jealousy and political intrigue prevented him receiving credit for success, resulting in his discharge. In 1790 he retired and lived in Paris, where he died and was subsequently buried. In 1905 his remains were removed from his long-forgotten grave and brought to the United States, escorted by four cruisers, where in 1913, he was finally re-interred in the US Naval Academy Chapel in Anapolis, Maryland.

JOHN PAUL JONES

Kirkcudbright's aye a Stewardry yet,
Not grouped as shire as fools wad jest.
Was not the first steward o' the earth
To work and till the garden sent?
A steward-like nation once were we,   5
As rulers named on trust perceived,
But silent tears, with yon cause lost,
Fell by the year this boy was born.
This lad's employ of first, aged twelve,
Was cabin boy, then first mate when   10
To merchant slavers' ships on ocean,
Their section gave him quick promotion.
When this man took first real command,
He killed a mutineer then ran
Far off, with burning hopes retracted,   15
So on his surname, Jones he added.
Negating George the Third's taxation
Which sarely long disturbed the nations,
When one of those did surely sever,
Joined John Paul Jones with fullest fervour,   20
To truly prove his bent as captain,
In moves with *Providence* here harken:
A score, less four of prize ships taken,
And Nova Scotia's bastions shaken,
Then France to sail a sloop named *Ranger*,   25
Whose flag they'd hail as new gained neighbours.
Then daring trips to bring his birlinns,
Not sparing ships near brink o' Britain.
With veterans in merged fleet fleet,
Americans with French to lead.   30
At sea, a lot he won with might.
Said he, 'I've not begun the fight'
Though twenty craft or more war took,
America, John Jones forsook.
When envy then, a rift did make,   35
Though pledged to help, Catherine the Great.
As admiral of her feared navy,
That man did fall to intrigue sarely.
Though laid in France he'd end his days,
In Maryland interred he stays.   40

15 HELEN GLOAG 1750–c.1790

Born near Muthill in Perthshire, Helen Gloag was brought up in a place that was subdued and poverty stricken as a result of the failure of the last Jacobite Rising.

She decided to leave for Carolina to seek a better life. But on the journey Helen and all on board were taken captive by pirates from Morocco, who were known for their extreme cruelty.

Although bought by a merchant and sold to the Sultan for his harem, her beauty was to make her the Empress of Morocco, which brought dramatic changes to that society through her influence, which is evident still to this day.

Glossary/Explication

LINES 1–3 Lord Drummond – Lord Strathallan, the Duke of Perth, was Chief of Clan Drummond and also the Jacobite laird of South Perthshire. He died from his wounds received at Culloden in 1746. See also Robert Burns (19) – notes on LINES 11–12. Marshall law imposed after the Jacobite rising of 1745.

LINES 4–7 Helen (aged 19) and friends sailed from Greenock in 1769.

LINES 8–14 The vessel had been at sea for only a few weeks when it was attacked by a pack of feared xebecs. These swift three-masted ships of 200 tons carried many guns and the fearsome pirates of Salle, Morocco, who hated European Christians. Salle was where they had their base and a school of pilots and pirates. A sandbar at the harbour mouth allowed them to enter and not be pursued.

LINES 15–21 What happened to the men and most of the women is unspeakable. The beautiful Helen was taken to the slave market where a sharp-eyed merchant paid a fortune for her and then presented her to the Grand Vizier, the Abdullah, the ruler of Morocco. He quickly made Helen his fourth wife and raised her to the status of Empress.

LINES 21–32 Helen's influence over her husband halted shipping of Negro slaves from Morocco (by the English, according to her own letters). British captives were let go unmolested, and even the Salle pirates were legally abolished. Trading deals and agreements were sealed with the British, and in 1782 assistance was given to them for their Battle of Gibraltar, keeping it under British control.

LINES 33–36 The Sultan built towns for trading purposes, such as his Atlantic port of Mogador, now called Essaoira, which brought traders from all over Europe. Here massively long camel caravans came from far inland to sell their wares.

LINES 37–39 Helen had two sons and frequently sent many communications home via her sea-captain brother Robert. But when her husband died, he had nominated a nephew to succeed him. Unfortunately, his cousin's mad half-son (to a German concubine), Yazeed, raised a revolt against his father causing yet again another reign of unspeakable terror in Morocco. To escape Yazeed's reign, Helen sent her sons to a Christian monastery in the town of Teuten, but Yazeed's troops ravaged the town and more than likely killed the two princes.

LINES 39–40 Helen's fate is unknown. However, a statue of the Scottish Empress stands in Rabat, Morocco.

HELEN GLOAG

Lord Drummond, due to winds o' strife
Was summoned to the prince's side.
His land subdued with brutal laws,
A lass fae Muthill took the call,
Embarking sprightly, her intent   5
For Carolina, with her friends
To sail there for a freer life,
But barely thought she'd see this sight:
From Ship's masthead, 'Corsairs' 'twas cried.
The Christians' dread was sarely tried.   10
So captured by the Moors and taken
To Salle, sae frightened, poor and shaken,
Her friends, she'd never see again,
Lives spent sae ever near to death.
A merchant of the market bought her   15
As present for the Grand Abdulla.
Her green eyes with her gold red hair
Would be prized gift to hold their stare.
Two thousand strong was Sultan's harem,
There housed not long would this lass tarry,   20
For he then pressed her hand in marriage,
As real Empress to have advantage
O'er hellish cruelty in those places,
Would Helen truly win more changes.
When Negro slave laws were extinguished,   25
Said she, ''Twas trade that served the English.'
When British captives were released,
Then minished, pirates' daring deeds.
Fair trade and treaties would this alter
With aid far reaching through Gibraltar.   30
As spoil for Britain to be gained,
Whose soil long with it too remained.
Port Mogador's new centre grew up
For hordes to call from Western Europe,
Where caravans of wax and carpets   35
On camels' backs, unpacked at markets.
When Sultan died, Yazeed ascended
Her sons demised where he descended
But what's ne'er kent by sage nor abbot:
The Scottish Empress reigns in Rabat.   40

16 THOMAS SMITH 1752–1815

Thomas Smith was born in Ferryport in Fife, the son of a mariner. When his father drowned at sea, he chose not to follow the same career.

Instead, he worked in Edinburgh, developing the street lighting, where he perfected his own reflecting lamp, which he mass produced. He became principal lighting engineer of the Northern Lighthouse Board. He was master of the city's ancient Incorporation of Hammermen.

He married three times. His third wife was Joan, a widowed mother. He passed his skills on to her son, Robert Stevenson, sowing the seed for what was to become the Stevenson lighthouse dynasty.

Glossary/Explication

LINES 1–4 It would ultimately be the Stevenson lighthouses that would, in hindsight, be the result of Thomas Smith's invention and the development of his reflecting lamps, coupled with the marriage to the widowed Jean Stevenson, whose son was Robert Stevenson (his apprentice), plus his introduction of lighting of seamarks to the dangerous coasts of Scotland and the Isle of Man.

LINE 6 *Mair* – more (Scots). 'Beam' – the lighthouse beam.

LINES 7–8 Until the coming of lighthouses, hill bonfires were used on prominent places as warnings for ships, the disadvantage being that they could be extinguished by extreme weather.

LINES 9–10 Both he and his father were called Thomas. Since Thomas's father had been a mariner who drowned at sea young, Thomas decided not to follow the same career. *Sare bent* – sore inclination (Scots).

LINES 13–14 Cairn of Dundee, the name of the first company who employed him, but he didn't stay long with them.

LINES 15–16 It was not long before he moved south to Edinburgh, where opportunity abounded. *Tak' sae* – take so (Scots). 'Auld Reekie' – Scots nickname for Edinburgh.

LINES 17–20 The Edinburgh street lighting. By the 1780s, he had taken an interest in reflectors – at that time concerned with street lighting. He then perfected his own reflecting lamps, which would be his hallmark, or 'seal-stamp'.

LINES 23–26 When the Northern Lighthouse Board was set up, he found himself not only principal lighting engineer, but also its first consultant. Hence he set this 'sphere in writing', i.e. documented.

LINES 27–28 This system was more effective than the open bonfires. See notes on LINES 1–4 and LINE 7 above. He stayed in the far North all the while.

LINES 29–36 The Incorporation of Hammermen was founded in 1483 for craftsmen. He became Master of that ancient corporation. *Sae muckle* – so big or manifold (Scots).

LINES 37–40 See Notes on LINES 1–4 above, and also Robert Stevenson (29).

THOMAS SMITH

True testimonies all re-beckon,
Blue crests in many, on reflection,
Whose legacy o' beacons shine,
And decorate our seacoast line.
For them, thank God, all seamen must,   5
And mair that awesome beam there trust.
But bonfire lights on fickle winds,
In long nights might all this rescind.
When Thomas Smith did drown at sea,
Went all his kindred down with grief,   10
But tramping off his namesake went,
Not backing though, that same sare bent.
But Cairn he went with in Dundee,
And fair apprenticeship but gleaned,
Then strides he'd tak' sae big or breezy   15
To wider markets in Auld Reekie.
But light defection to these streets
Brought bright reflections to be seen,
Selecting he, as his real stamp,
New lenses clear to build clear lamps.   20
As honest tinsmith and inventor,
He'd en masse build his lamp reflectors,
When Northern Lighting was set up,
This Scotsman rightly won their trust.
Then often set this sphere in writing,   25
As top-rank engineer in lighting,
For seamarks he'd plot round the coasts,
But keep that keen north's ground his post.
His ancient, purest art as crafter,
Would take him to the mark of master,   30
To Hammermen's Incorporation,
Whose arts were kent in all our nation,
With men who forged thick silver buckles,
For weapons, swords smiths skilled sae muckle,
With gold-smiths, black-smiths, jewellers, culters,   35
Who'd mould drink tankards pewter covered.
Jean Stevenson was his third wife,
Whose genius son would fill his life
With effervescent beams tae shine out,
Whose legacy would be the lighthouse.   40

17 SIR JOHN SINCLAIR 1754–1835

Laird of Ulbster, Caithness, and educated in Glasgow, Edinburgh and Oxford, Sinclair became an advocate in both England and Scotland and travelled abroad.

He was a follower of the Enlightenment, and became a Member of Parliament. He was appointed the first President of the Board of Agriculture and introduced the Cheviot sheep into Caithness to help the farmers improve the quality of their lives, but his idea was turned against him by greedy neighbours.

He started the enormous task of compiling the first statistical survey of the country. He wrote the Statistical Account of Scotland, *confronting the conscience of the nation.*

Glossary/Explication

LINES 1–2 'Dunniewassal' – pronounced 'dooniwassal', from the Gaelic, *duine-uasal*. Also known as 'tacksman', he was the mediator between the chief or chieftain and the cotter, whom he could call out as a military force.

LINE 4 The Enlightenment was a period in history where modern scientific thinking and reasoning was born.

LINES 5–10 He graduated as an advocate from Glasgow, Edinburgh and Oxford universities. After travelling widely abroad he became an MP in 1780.

LINES 11–14 His culture being, in this case, the lot of the farmers around him in his native Caithness. He founded the Department of Agriculture during William Pitt the Younger's government.

LINES 15–18 'Grades of gauging' – see notes on LINES 33–38 below. His firm conviction was that trews, rather than the kilt or plaid, was the original dress of the Highlander, as in his excellent portrait by Henry Raeburn. LINE 17 *Mak'* – make (Scots). LINE 18 'Trews' (Gaelic *triubhas*) – Hose like a tight fitting lower body stocking of tartan cloth cut on the bias for pliability. As opposed to *trousers*, which are simply breeks albeit some of them designed in tartan.

LINES 19–20 The Proscription Act of 1747, which banned the wearing of Highland dress.

LINE 21–24 *a'chaorach mhor* – the great sheep (Gaelic). The Cheviot was a special hardy border breed. John's intention was for this breed to help the people prosper.

LINES 25–26 An adaptation of the Biblical declaration, 'The love of money is the root of all evil'. *Siller:* silver (Scots).

LINE 27 The Marquis of Stafford, or Duke of Sutherland, of 'Highland Clearances' infamy.

LINE 30 Patrick Sellar was Stafford's brutal factor and ethnic cleanser.

LINES 31–32 Reflecting colonial policy against the Gael, as with the American Indian.

LINES 33–38 In 1791, he started compiling the first statistical survey for the nation, about its economic, social and natural resources, gaining a measure of 'the quantum of happiness' of communities as a means of future improvement. Questionnaires were distributed to ministers in almost 1,000 parishes, including 160 questions, ranging from ethics to climate. Those reluctant ministers were pursued until they submitted all sought information, which was then collected and collated in his mammoth *Statistical Account of Scotland* – 21 volumes in all!

LINES 39–40 John's ideas of improvements were intended to help people stay and prosper on their land. *Hames* – homes (Scots).

SIR JOHN SINCLAIR

A high-born dashing dunniewassal,
With plight of farmers viewed as vassals,
Imbued with heightened sense of pride did,
The New Enlightenment then side with.
In Glasgow and in Edinburgh,   5
This man so ardent, well did further
The frontiers of his mind and thought
Through some years from his time abroad.
MP and advocate with flare,
Would be that star o' wit, Sinclair.   10
To more advance his culture's cause,
The Board of Agriculture was
For him as first Chair, there for taking,
In William Pitt's days, ever changing.
Collating information made him   15
A sage within all grades of gauging.
He'd state to patrons' views so spartan,
Whilst bravely wearing trews of tartan,
Although in law nigh still proscribed,
He those did don, by his old right.   20
For bad or good, new great sheep came,
Whose hardihood could make real gain,
Promote fairness for folks around
Remote Caithness where scores abound.
But love o' siller's e'er the reason   25
For worldly ills, in every season.
For Stafford took then John's good seed
To plant full forests sown through greed.
In that sick hell, burned strangest fires,
And Patrick Sellar's name despised.   30
The empire's sinful gravest greed,
Would exile its own bravest breed.
So bold surveys John started then,
For 'quantum (state) of happiness'.
In clergy names then of a thousand,   35
Which questionnaires, them all astounded,
For figures and amounts then hidden,
On statistical accounts were written.
So for the shells o' cotters' hames,
Sir John himself must not be blamed.   40

18 WILLIAM MURDOCH 1754–1839

Born in Lugar in Ayrshire, William Murdoch walked to Birmingham and apprenticed himself to James Watt, who at that time was in partnership with Boulton.

William improved the steam engine by adding the slide valve and sun and planet wheels, while he upgraded the Bell crank engine. But his greatest contribution to mankind, by far for its day, was the 'cockspur', the first gas light, which he used to light his house, factory and the streets of London.

He also invented the steam car. Pneumatic power by compressed air would eventually bring about lifts and even domestic doorbells.

Glossary/Explication

LINE 1 'Stunning style' – see notes on LINES 5–7 below.

LINES 5–7 Totally committed to becoming an apprentice of James Watt, he walked 300 miles to Birmingham. At the outset of the interview he placed his makeshift hat on the table, which, it transpires, was turned from wood. Watt and his partner Boulton were so impressed by Murdoch's wit and inventiveness that they took him on. *Skelf* – wooden splinter (Scots).

LINES 8–9 Boulton and Watt sent Murdoch to oversee their engines being installed at the tin mines in Cornwall. See also James Watt (13).

LINE 13 Slide valve – for channelling steam in and out. Mostly used on steam engines.

LINES 17–28 Monologue I've made up in rhyme illustrating his gas lighting 'cockspur' invention. LINE 21 *Feartie* – a coward (Scots). LINE 28 The cockspur – the name of the first gas light.

LINES 29–30 Heating peat, coal and wood in the absence of air, he stored the gases given off, and used them to light his house in 1792. Thirteen years later, his factory was lit by gas. See also Charles Macintosh (27) – note on LINE 22.

LINES 31–32 By 1807, London's streets were being lit by gas, making it safer for people going out at night.

LINES 33–36 He housed a steam engine on a wheeled frame, which he drove through the streets of Redruth in Cornwall.

LINES 37–40 'Compressed air' – using air pressure to move parcels in hollow funnels. This method was used widely in industry within living memory, and efficiently quickened communications within industrial buildings. At the Boulton and Watt works this power base energised and lifted moulded products from the factory base, hoisting them up to the nearby canal bank for transportation. For his very own house, he installed compressed air to power the doorbells to ring.

WILLIAM MURDOCH

To Birmingham's streets, stunning style
Which distance spans three hundred miles,
Walked this keen boy, and knowledge sought,
At the feet of that Scot, James Watt.
A wooden hat he turned himself   5
Sae smoothly that he'd pluck nae skelf.
His mind o' skills, James so impressed.
To mines o' tin he'd show him next,
In Cornwall, to lay installations,
Yet for all, he'd make innovations.   10
Steam engines smartly Will built better,
And then in partnership linked tethered.
Though slide valves, sun and planet wheels,
Which guide and turn that arm of steel,
With Bell crank engine too upgraded,   15
His next invention would upstage it.
Well 'twas a joy though getting wiser,
Yet as a boy coal mesmerised him.
''Tis more than solid pyre,' he reckoned,
'Its glory or its ire let's beckon.'   20
No feartie though, Will aye had mettle,
So heated coal inside a kettle.
Its spout filled o'er thumbed o'er wi' thimble,
Drilled out with holes drummed out sae nimble.
From coal, peat, and wood without air,   25
His stored sealed gas would fling out flares.
From three wee notches flames aye breathing,
The cheery cockspur sprayed fire seething.
His factory and house this lit up,
Which afterwards did soundly stir up   30
A revolution spurred like lightning,
Whose debut route was London's lighting.
In comely Cornwall's fairest Redruth,
The public saw what made the best news.
On streets therein, their cheers declaimed,   35
His steam engine in three wheel frame.
And thinking of high commerce there,
Transmitting power by compressed air
Would propel brand new static lifts
And doorbells as pneumatic gifts.   40

19 ROBERT BURNS 1759–1796

Born in Alloway, Rabbie Burns, our national Bard, is celebrated in Scotland and, indeed, all over the world.

His hard life was curtailed when he died at the age of 37 through rheumatic fever, contracted simply through all the hardships of farming life. This great struggling artist took up the post of excise-man, but his illnesses finally got the better of him.

In spite of all that, he left us with three great anthems: the first, the patriotic and nationalist 'Scots Wha Hae'; and the other two for all of mankind, 'Auld Lang Syne' and 'A Man's a Man for A' That'.

Glossary/Explication

Most lines are titles of his poems/songs and are composed in the form of an 'acrostic', reading down the left side –

RABBIE-BURNS-A-MANS-A-MAN-FOR-A-THAT-AULD-LANG-SYNE, denoting his name and two of his anthems.

LINES 1–2 'Rantin' Rovin' Robin' and 'A Bard's Epitaph' reflect Rabbie's own tempestuous life.

LINES 3–4 'Braving Angry Winter Storms' – an ode to Peggy set in the Ochils. 'Book-Worms' – a four-line satire.

LINES 5–6 'It Was a' for Oor Rightfu' King' – a Jacobite song.

LINES 7–8 He was a very patriotic bard, during a period when such notions were seen as treasonable.

LINES 9–10 'Robert's March to Bannockburn', i.e. 'Scots Wha Hae', was another brave song, and was our national anthem until the early 1970s.

LINES 11–12 'Strathallan's Lament' – The feelings of Strathallan (Drummond, Duke of Perth), who died in France from wounds received at Culloden. 'Awa' Whigs Awa" – a political dirge lamenting the passing of the Scots Stewart dynasty.

LINES 13–14 'Man was Made to Mourn' – a lengthy dirge. 'A Mother's Lament' – for the death of her son.

LINES 15–16 'Sic Parcel o' Rogues' – a song against the 1707 Union of Parliaments, blaming the swaying bankrupt lairds and politicians.

LINES 17–24 He composed charming and noble eulogies praising womankind. See LINES 35–37.

LINES 25–26 He collected the chorus of 'Highland Harry Back Again' from an old woman in Dunblane, but added verses himself, reflecting the people's undying loyalty to Bonnie Prince Charlie.

LINES 27–28 'Tam o' Shanter' – a tremendous epic spooky ceilidh or party piece. A tale well told in rhyming couplets, in 200 lines.

LINES 29–32 'A Man's a Man for a' That' – echoing the French revolution, this song extols honesty far above rank and privilege.

LINES 33–34 'Auld Lang Syne' – the New Year song, the most international ever sung, heartily expresses that 'water under the bridge' attitude, mirroring an inherited hearty Celtic armistice.

LINES 35–37 'Green Grows the Rashes O' – see note on LINES 17–24 above.

LINES 38–40 'A Man's a Man for a' That', was sung on the day of the Scottish Parliament's opening in 1999 by Sheena Wellington. That same year that a human rights bill was passed by Parliament. How appropriate!

ROBERT BURNS

R ab's Rantin' Rovin' Robin o's
A bard's ain poem or song o' yore,
B orne Braving Angry Winter Storms,
B erating artless imp book-worms.
I t Was a' for Oor Rightfu' King's,   5
E voking songs whose likes he'd sing.
B urlesque and boldly, Rob did write,
U nearthing solely Scotland's plight.
R oused Robert's March to Bannockburn,
N e'er from did Rabbie that cause turn.   10
S trathallan's passing o' Fifteen,
A wa Whigs A', did hold this clear.
M an (just) Was Made to Mourn, no doubt.
A mother's wailing woes would shout.
N oised Rab with coarse deliberation –   15
S ic 'Parcel o' Rogues' in a nation.
A nd lassies' herts he'd steal, disarmin',
M use makin' e'er wi' cheerfu' charmin'.
A Red Red Rose, stowed stout o' passion, 's
N ot yet an ode so out o' fashion.   20
F arewell to Ballochmyle, compares wi'
O Wert my Love Yon Lilac Fair, wi',
R ued Ravin Winds Around Her Blowing,
A ppraising with a proud imploring.
T hough rhymes did Rabbie add to end,   25
H ailed Highland Harry Back Again,
A phantom saga, charmed, enchanted,
T all Tam o' Shanter, Rabbie crafted.
A Man's a Man For a' That truly,
U nravelled facts about hard ruling   30
L ang lauding all o' Adam's bairnies,
D efrocking all in rank then reigning.
L ang oft do chime New Year's, foo' glasses,
A s Auld Lang Syne fou cheers the masses.
N eat odes o' passion's road wrote Rabbie,   35
G reen Grow the Rashes O' goes aptly
S ung out at banquets and poor hames,
Y et now! A Man's a Man's oor ain
N ew nation's parliamentary rhyme,
E quating apt with, Auld Lang Syne.   40

20 ALEXANDER MacGILLIVRAY 1750–1793

Of the line of the House of Dunmaglas, Alexander MacGillivray was probably the nephew of Colonel Alexander MacGillivray, Captain of Clan Chattan, who fell, but acquitted himself with great honour, at the Battle of Culloden on 16 April 1746.

In America, Alexander, a brilliant politician, became the elected leader of the Creek Nation. He was one of the numerous High-landers who became native American leaders.

This superbly talented diplomat negotiated with President George Washington, succeeding over decades in maintaining Creek inde-pendence by constantly switching support from one to another of the three great white powers – Spain, Britain and the United States.

Glossary/Explication

LINES 1–14 From an incident on Culloden Field. Colonel Alexander MacGillivray's battalion made the furious attack at Culloden that almost annihilated the left wing of the Duke of Cumberland's army, but he lost his life, along with four officers of his clan. This brave soldier encountered the commander of Barrel's regiment, and struck off some of the English Colonel's fingers with his broadsword. After the conflict was over, MacGillivray was stripped, and his waistcoat, undoubtedly handsomely embroidered, was appropriated by a private soldier. Walking along the streets of Inverness in his garment, the private was met by Barrel's Colonel who indignantly stopped the man, and ordered him immediately to take it off. 'I recognise that waistcoat,' said the generous warrior, 'I met on the field of battle the brave man who wore it, and it shall not now be thus degraded.'

LINES 15–16 Cattan, after whom Clan Chattan is named. This was a great federation of clans whose symbol is the cat, including the MacGillivrays, the MacPhersons, the MacIntoshes, the MacBains and the Farquarsons.

LINES 17–20 This Alexander MacGillivray was thought to be the nephew of the said Colonel above, although some say that he may have been a MacDonald who changed his name. LINE 19 See also notes on LINES 23–34 below.

LINES 21–22 Their dilemma was that they, like the Cherokee, would try and gain some kind of nationhood or autonomy. Therefore, as outlined in the subsequent couplets, they had to make treaties with all the incoming super powers, whilst keeping their dignity intact. Their own tribe was also divided in its loyalties. See also notes on LINES 23–34 below.

LINES 23–34 George Washington was the President at the time. Highlanders and Indians shared their plights empathetically. The ethic of property over people was over-running both cultures virtually simultaneously, therefore it was easy for dispossessed Highlanders to become Native Americans. Numerous tribes or nations ended up being led by Highlanders, such as the Nez Perce by Angus MacDonald and the Cherokee by John Ross. See also (Jarl) Henry Sinclair (1), Sir Alexander Mackenzie (24), John Ross (Cherokee) (39), William Drummond Stewart (41) and David Douglas (43). In Scotland, many clansmen were in the same dilemma, i.e. what should come first, loyalty to nationhood (Scotland's sovereignty) or clan?

LINES 35–40 See notes on LINES 21–22 above.

ALEXANDER MacGILLIVRAY

'I recognise that waistcoat!' said,
A Redcoat's high and gracious head.
'I faced him on the field of battle,
Who braved the storm with steel and mantle.'
'Leave him alone!' then I commanded,   5
'For even though my hand he damaged,
And seven of my men he conquered,
And fell then by that well of slaughter.
Degraded thus, that shall not be,
Remain it must in charge with me.'   10
There for a soldier, this he said,
Who donned that spoil in Inverness.
This colonel, at Culloden faced
A colonel of another race,
Of worthy Cattan's patrimony,   15
A Dunmaglas man, aye sae worthy.
But geared to lead across wild oceans,
And reared with Creeks old tribe's devotions,
As Cherokees adhered to Gaels thus,
This fellow chief achieved good status.   20
Superbly talented, that elder,
Would thereby highlight their dilemma.
With Washington, well stood he fast,
Whilst calling him next to the task
Of independence of his nation   25
Whilst in real heavy confrontation
With various white powers at times,
This brave did just right out align
With Britain, USA or Spain,
And skilful moves sustain or gain,   30
The better interests for his folk
As threatened kinsmen sought at home
Where dominant regimes in waves,
Did prominently keep the sway,
And each invested and there had   35
Strategic interests in their land.
But more division, cleaved his tribesmen,
By sore seditious deals with white men,
But treaties, fought hard he to keep,
While seeking for that people's peace.   40

21 THOMAS TELFORD 1757–1834

A shepherd's son from Westerkirk, Dumfries, Thomas Telford, perceiving that society was rapidly changing, took his skills as a mason to Edinburgh where the New Town was being built.

His obvious talents took him to Shropshire in the south-west of England, where a new town was named after him. As surveyor and engineer, he built 1,200 bridges as well as over 1,000 miles of road in the Highlands. He also built the Caledonian Canal, the then world's longest bridge, and a giant aqueduct in Wales.

He was the world's first consultant engineer, who raised standards for building contractors thereafter.

Glossary/Explication

LINES 1–6 Thomas worked as a shepherd boy and herdsman in the peaceful wilds of Dumfries-shire then learned his new craft as a stonemason.

LINES 7–10 'Laughing Tam' – his nickname. In the early 1780s he quickly found work in Edinburgh's New Town as a stonemason crafting splendid frontages.

LINES 11–12 As an engineer he was Surveyor of Public Works in Shropshire, and Telford New Town is named after him.

LINES 13–14 George Wade was a General in the English (and eventually British) Army commissioned to 'pacify' the Jacobite Highlands by building a string of roads, bridges and forts between the Jacobite Risings of 1715 and 1745. Arguably, Telford's work was a continuation of Wade's, whose construction of roads, bridges and even churches made the Highlands more accessible. See also John Loudon McAdam (25).

LINES 15–18 *Coinneach Odhar* (Gaelic) – pronounced 'Koinyuch owar', meaning 'Sallow Kenneth', was known as the 'Braan Seer'. He was Kenneth Mackenzie, who foretold, amongst many things, of the coming of the Caledonian Canal, which Telford built.

LINES 19–22 In 1793, as engineer for the Ellesmere Canal Company, he built a canal over two deep river valleys. A staggering achievement, the Pontcysyllte (pronounced 'Pont-kye-sighlty' in South Wales is the longest and highest aqueduct in Britain.

LINES 23–26 The centre of the road raised to drain off water. He also scrutinised chip size for smoothness – see John Loudon McAdam (25). His first route was London to Holyhead in north-west Wales, en route to Ireland.

LINES 27–28 The suspension bridge across the Menia Straights to Anglesey is a world-famous structure that still carries traffic, and claimed then to be the world's longest bridge and first ever suspension bridge.

LINES 29–32 King Gustav knighted Telford for the Gota Canal, which runs from Lake Malaren (Stockholm) to Lakes Vaner and Vettir.

LINES 35–40 As the first professional civil engineer, he demanded that all contracts be clearly written, hence 'on track handling' in LINE 37 (double entendre for the new railway age to come). He improved the quality standards of building contractors, recruiting willing trainees to become 'Telford trained', reaching the top in the railway age. He founded the Institute of Civil Engineering in 1818.

THOMAS TELFORD

In Westerkirk, by green Dumfries,
The shepherd's work ne'er pierced the peace
Nor solace in those rolling hills,
Where Thomas firstly honed his skills.
But yet he laid this up at last   5
To learn the mason's cunning craft.
So Laughing Tam did reach Auld Reekie,
To carve his brand sae keenly, clearly
On looming towering spacious spaces
Of New Town houses' stately faces.   10
His engineering's e'er renowned,
And well revered in Telford town.
But Laughing Tam, on George Wade's tail
Made pathways tracking on his trail.
Twelve hundred bridges, stout and stylish   15
Linked up within a thousand miles with
Lang bonnie roads, canals to mould,
As *Coinneach Odhar* had foretold.
His hardest truss and longest line is
The aqueduct of Pontcysyllte,   20
With cast iron troughs to take the weight,
This was high country's bravest brace.
The middle of his roads he raised,
To rid them of the pouring rain.
So horse could tread so dry with grip   25
Through Holyhead, for Ireland's trip
Which meant a trip on Tam's invention –
Aye Menai's bridge of hard suspension.
This engineering's guid consultant
Did get the Swedish King's resultant   30
First contract, charter, draft for building
For Gota Canal's plans fulfilling.
New railway groups then sought his vision,
Preparing routes well wrought with wisdom.
As civil engineer, first ever,   35
That gifted man did steer in clever
New ways to purvey on-track handling,
Through great new survey contracts planning.
New generations came to hone them,
Aye Telford Trained!, proclaimed their slogan.   40

Born in Ulva, adjacent to Mull, and related to the chief of his clan,
Lachlan MacQuarrie left home whilst young and joined the army,
where he served and acquitted himself with honour in America,
Canada, Egypt and India.

Rising to the rank of lieutenant-colonel, he was appointed to take
over the position of the infamous William Bligh of Bounty fame, as
Governor of New South Wales, Australia. Immediately on taking
up this post, he began to assist in rehabilitating the continually
incoming convicts there, ultimately resulting in his dismissal.

He is regarded as the Founding Father to all Australians.

Glossary/Explication

LINES 1–2 Both of those Inner Hebridean islands are collectively mountainous.

LINES 3–4 Lachlan's father was cousin to the 16th and last chief of the Clan MacQuarrie of Ulva.

LINES 7–8 Now living on Mull, he joined the army at the age of 15 in 1776.

LINES 9–10 In 1777 he obtained an ensign in the 2nd battalion the 84th Regiment, known as the Royal Highland Emigrants, and served in Canada at Halifax and other parts of Nova Scotia.

LINES 11–20 He was commissioned a lieutenant in the 71st Regiment in 1781, serving in New York and Charleston at the closing of the American War of Independence. In 1787, in the 77th Regiment in India, he saw much action in seven battles and sieges. In March 1801, as Governor of Bombay, MacQuarrie was appointed deputy-adjutant-general to the 8,000-strong army sent to Egypt to expel the French. They marched 140 miles across the desert from the Red Sea coast of Cossier to Keneh. From there they sailed down the Nile to Cairo before reaching Alexandria. In 1803 Lachlan returned to Britain to dine with the king and queen and had his portrait painted in London by John Opie, a noted Cornish artist of the time, whilst on his way home to Scotland. In Scotland he re-married to Henrietta Campbell of Airds, his distant cousin.

LINE 21–34 As Governor of New South Wales, Australia he replaced the cruel William Bligh of *Bounty* fame. With an increased number of convicts incoming, Lachie's solution was to commence a programme of public works and a ticket-of-leave for convicts. This brought him into conflict with the influential conservative 'exclusives' who sought to restrict civil rights and judicial privileges. Many of these settlers also had influential friends in English political circles. See also Alexander Maconochie (36).

LINES 35–38 Frustration and bouts of illness led him to submit his resignation. Although he came nearby his native island of Ulva, he was buried on Mull itself, on the Jarvisfield estate, then owned by him (possibly named after his first wife, Jane Jarvis).

LINES 39–40 He is regarded as the Founding Father of Australia.

LACHLAN MacQUARRIE

From Mull and Ulva of the bens,
And worthy sturdy solid men,
A Gael of manful chieftain's seed,
Though raised of mannered low degree,
Yet left his native Ulva, early,   5
And escapades begun as well wi'
Bold volunteering aged fifteen,
To join war theatre's raging scene.
With emigrants, he'd make his corps,
The Regiment of Eighty Fourth,   10
Then come next out with, till truce-talks,
Another outfit in New York.
In Egypt with eight thousand troops,
He'd lead them in great routs, and routes.
In India he'd settle troubles,   15
With skill in arms, in seven struggles.
Through Bombay, homewards Lachie journeyed,
To bond in restful matrimony,
Where Opie captured all on canvas,
Before departure for his last task   20
As Governor of New South Wales
Uncovering cold cruel fowl ways
Through scrutiny, and highest courage,
For mutiny, had Bligh erupted.
'A penal jail!' exclaim did Lachie,   25
'Will really make this place unhappy.
My view then for uneven ways is
Improvement for more equal status,
With modern towns and roads to build,
The convicts now can hone good skills.'   30
But discord with the Anglo-settlers,
Ill-will brought him in angry letters.
For share they dared not Lachie's vision,
Who made that caring plan his mission.
Through ailment, he resigned that post,   35
And came next near his island's coast.
Though that is clear here is inferred,
In Jarvisfield, he is interred.
This architect-humanitarian,
Is father yet to all Australians.   40

23 WILLIAM MacLURE 1763–1840

Born in Ayr, William MacLure came from a wealthy family who had business interests in import and export.

His wealth allowed him to give his life to philanthropic interests. On returning to America where he had been as a child, he took up US citizenship and presidency of Philadelphia's Academy of Natural Sciences.

After several visits to Europe, he became interested in geology and began his epic journey through every state in the United States, working on what was to be America's first ever geology map.

He also financed the New Harmony utopian experiment and New Lanark Mills project, which was based upon co-operative ideals.

Glossary/Explication

LINES 1–4 MacLure is spelled in the original Gaelic, *Clann 'ill-leabhair*, pronounced 'Clown eel leywair', meaning 'the children of the book servant'. According to tradition, the MacLures were the hereditary scribes and tutors to MacLeod of Dunvegan on the Isle of Skye, off the west coast of Scotland. The 'children of the book servant' is therefore a name which is a title or a right.

LINES 5–10 The New World was then the place with new ideals and opportunity.

LINES 11–16 In 1803 MacLure served in Paris on a United States commission, representing American citizens on the French government with losses resulting from the French Revolution. Having conducted geological studies in France and Spain, he began intensive studies in the United States in 1808. In 1812 he was to become a member of the newly-founded Academy of Natural Sciences of Philadelphia (ANSP), and in 1817 became its president, a post which he was to hold for the next 22 years. LINE 12 – 'in that state' refers to Virginia.

LINES 17–26 In 1807, on return home from his first visit to France, he began the self-imposed task of making a geological survey of the United States. Almost every state in the union was to be traversed by him, the Allegheny Mountains being crossed and recrossed some 50 times. The results of his labours were submitted to the American Philosophical Society in a memoir entitled *Observations of the United States explanatory of a Geological Map*, and published in the Society's *Transactions*, together with the first geological map of that country. He also brought before them a revised edition of his map, and his great geological memoir was issued separately with some additional matter under the title *Observations on the Geology of the United States of America*.

LINES 27–30 His geological map antedates William Smith's geological map of England by six years.

LINES 37–38 He funded the utopian community of New Harmony, Indiana, which Robert Owen (who had bought it from George Rapp, the Harmonist leader) founded upon idealistic and radical management of the mills in New Lanark by the Firth of Clyde. Therefore, New Harmony was the teacher and New Lanark its ultimate manifestation.

LINE 40 He is regarded as the Father of Geology of the USA.

WILLIAM MacLURE

What's in a name, as in MacLure?
A link with papers this assures.
For *Clann 'ill-leabhair* claim the right,
As grand Dunvegan's ancient scribes.
That calling came for this rough rover,   5
Who born in Ayr but did come over
The wild Atlantic to Virginia,
Where wide advantage could begin a
Fair chance to trade in that duration,
Where vast new ways would carve new nations.   10
In London yet he'd rin affairs,
But upped and settled in that state,
Then came o'er next, as sought by France,
For claims to settle, not by chance.
Whilst on long stay he'd take in Europe,   15
Geology became his true work,
Then William came back to the States,
To willingly and truly traipse
Or tramp through trails in free traverse,
To map those states frae east to west,   20
Then chart them well frae south to north
And Allegheny's mountains cross,
Some fifty times yon range to study
Through rifts and climbs for sake o' surveys,
Which memoirs and all observations,   25
Would serve as charts for all their nation.
Geology, his map highlighted,
Seen for its day first as far sighted,
Though England's first that anti-dated,
Saw William Smith's as antiquated.   30
The radical ideas of Owen,
Did start to plant the seeds for sowing
In management's new skills and thrust
With backing, lent through William's purse.
New Harmony revered as teacher,   35
New Lanark's mills revealed as feature.
In those domains he is well kent,
And noble name he himself lent,
For Geology's cause, charting farther,
In all those states as Mapping Father.   40

Born in Stornoway, Alexander Mackenzie emigrated with his father firstly to New York, then to Montreal, where he worked in the fur trade for the North West Company.

With a small party he set out to find a route to the West Pacific Ocean, but after 40 days' toil ended up in the Arctic Ocean.

Four years later he and a small expedition set out from North Alberta westwards on a long and dangerous adventure. After their canoe was smashed on the Fraser River, with the help of the local Indians, they eventually came to the Northwest Passage.

Glossary/Explication

LINES 1–4 There are just as many Scots in Canada or in the USA as there are here at home. Highland Scots represent the third largest ethnic group in Canada.

LINES 5–6 'The Hero Age' lasted until the Battle of Culloden in April 1746, after which social and economic depression brought about emigration fever.

LINE 7 He came to New York with his father and went to school in Montreal, and in 1779 became involved in the fur trade, eventually working for the North West Company.

LINE 8 'Blue-hawk', from the Gaelic hero tale where the blue falcon is the greatest hunting bird with excellent vision. Here I have made it into the adjective 'blue-hawked'.

LINES 9–10 I've used the 'echo' and 'beckon' allegories highlighting empathetic parallels and plights of the Native American with the Scottish Highlander. See also (Jarl) Henry Sinclair (1), Alexander MacGillivray (20) and John Ross (Cherokee) (39) William Drummond Stewart (41) and David Douglas (43).

LINES 11–14 'Norwest' – the abbreviated term for the North West Company. His vocation was as pioneering explorer.

LINES 15–24 His first attempt from the trading post on Lake Athabasca, in what is now north Alberta, was in the summer of 1789. The river is called the Mackenzie. Unfortunately, he had reached not the Pacific, but the Arctic Ocean.

LINES 25–37 Four years later, the North West gave Mackenzie another chance. He and his crew set out in May 1793 from Fort Fork, but eventually the rapids of the Fraser River caused the canoe to capsize. The nine adventurers found themselves floundering in the raging waters. Exhausted, they rambled westwards for two weeks on foot over the Coast mountains, coming across the Bella Coola Indians, who gave them a ride in their canoes and took them to the arm of the Pacific Ocean.

LINE 38 'Where red Mac first did coat his carn' – with mixed vermilion and melted grease, producing a red shade, on the rocks of the Dean Channel shore, he wrote: *Alexander Mackenzie, from Canada, by land the twenty-second of July, one thousand seven hundred and ninety-three.*

LINE 40 Alexander Mackenzie was the first person to discover the Northwest Passage. In 1801 he published a book, *Voyages From Montreal*, which Thomas Jefferson's explorers of the west took with them three years later.

SIR ALEXANDER MacKENZIE

The Hebrides' most western isle,
Was said to be o' men exiled
Not Lewis, Barra, Rum or Eigg,
But newer land that's further west.
For reared and raised for emigration,   5
When Heroes' Age reached termination,
Through New York aimed at Montreal,
This blue-hawked Brainheart got the call
That echoed out in plaintive wilds,
And beckoned stout in native style.   10
Whilst Norwest was his starting station,
He sought yet for his grand vocation.
While exploration sought advantage,
His next location brought the chances.
In birch canoes from north Alberta,   15
He'd first plan routes in hotter weather.
So eight men with their Native wives,
The lake then river waves did strike,
To pummel like great slaves, their pacing,
Through summer light made sare their racing.   20
Till in the north aye that host claimed,
And river called by Mac's own name.
In forty days the fear was frantic,
Since salt declared the seas of Arctic!
To strike again, four years on next,   25
With nine hard men, our hero left
Fort Fork, and plied a lengthy lead
On a boat of five and twenty feet.
On heading westwards through Peace Waters,
Whose bends and stretches sure screeched often.   30
Through rocks and rapids' teeth so white,
They hauled that craft with gear o'er heights.
Through Fraser and MacGregors' Rivers,
Those brave men crashed as terror simmered.
To Bella Coola's folk they rambled,   35
Then their canoes did board and paddle,
To west Pacific Ocean's arm,
Where red, Mac first did coat his carn.
This Hebridean mover's zest,
Had led frae east in through the west.   40

25 JOHN LOUDON MCADAM 1765–1836

Though born in Ayrshire, John Loudon McAdam went to New York to work with his uncle, who was a merchant banker in the city. He also helped his uncle to form the Chamber of Commerce there.

When America declared itself to be independent, John, with the fortune he made, came back to Scotland and bought an Ayrshire estate. When he saw the dilapidated state of the roads and tracks there, he decided to upgrade them using, and further developing, the Roman principles of road building by rolling over layers of crushed chips of rock.

So he invented tar and became Surveyor-General.

Glossary/Explication

LINES 1–7 Virtually all kinds of roads worldwide are now macadamised.

LINE 8 The travelling people of Scotland have contributed so many traditional folk songs on the 'road' theme to the folk revival.

LINE 9–10 Adapted from an old limerick. George Wade was an English General who built the first roads and bridges throughout the Highlands for its 'pacification' in the 18th century. See also Thomas Telford (21).

LINES 13–18 John worked with his uncle, who was a New York merchant banker, but the American Declaration of Independence changed things drastically for him. The breaking away was helped by some Scots such as Robert Smith (9), John Witherspoon (10) and John Paul Jones (14). He himself felt obliged to leave the country.

LINES 19–30 This is a classic example of just how necessity is indeed the mother of invention. In this case, his foot slips down a pot-hole on one of his estate roads or tracks, so he decides to re-invent and further develop Roman principles of road building, except adding crushed chipped stones on top over-rolled, thus inventing Tar or Tarmac. He gave exact particulars for the size of the chips for their respective depths that so each sheath would be placed compressing the chips to mould together when a cartwheel or roller was passed over them, developing a smooth surface, yet with good traction. He worked on similar projects running concurrently with those of Thomas Telford's (21), such as road-side drainage.

LINE 32 The abbreviated form of Tar McAdam, Tarmac, is the internationally known term for metalled roads throughout the world.

LINES 33–36 McAdam was consultant to over 30 road trusts, and by the late 1820s he was appointed Surveyor General of the Metropolitan Roads of Great Britain. 'Macadamised' became the term he used, as this is how the first highway in the USA was baptised in 1822. He was offered a knighthood but turned it down.

LINE 37–38 Like the old saying, 'If it's a lie I'm telling you, then it was a lie that was told to me.' He of course made the world smaller by his roads.

LINES 39–40 Adapted nova-riddle for tar. 'Soles' refers to the soles of your feet when the tar is hot in summertime.

JOHN LOUDON MCADAM

By high road, low road, back or main,
By by-road, loan, slow traffic lane,
By sidewalks, highways fringed and paved,
Aye mile for mile trail trips man-made.
Those darkest Tarmac tracks for tramping,   5
For caravan wi' car for camping,
Wi' lively crack the winter long,
Inspires the travellers with the song.
When auld George Wade raised roads and bridges,
And fought yon bare-faced bold mad midges,   10
Did he not know nor ne'er did fear,
There'd be a more sought engineer?
Though John was raised a guid true Scot
At Commerce Chamber in New York,
Of which his uncle did the leading,   15
He quit that country, quickly fleeing.
Which for real freedom sought tae sever
Through auld beliefs o' Scots sae clever.
So from great finance saved and sent through,
An auld Ayrshire estate he rescued.   20
Whilst in that lot, his grip slid slipping,
For in a pot, his shin ditched dipping.
Said he, 'those Romans tried their best,
Their wee old roads and styles let's test.
By adding crunched split rocks ensuring   25
A standard crushed chip for procuring.
And lay the largest type beneath,
All placed in bands there like a sheath,
The wee-est parts near top for holding
Well-sealed with cartwheel over-rolling.'   30
For this, McAdam lent his brand-mark,
Which all track travellers ken as Tarmac.
Macadamised – to choose as by-name,
That man baptised his newest highway.
Yet knighthood honour ne'er did take,   35
As right true Scot, for service sake.
Since truth ne'er turns a tall tale taller,
A newer world did John make smaller,
Wi' sealed black stuff that scorches soles,
For wheels that turn across the globe.   40

Born in Paisley, Alexander Wilson became an apprentice weaver by Castle Semple and wrote poetry extolling the beauty of the birds there. He also composed poetry criticising weaver employers, which brought him fines and jail sentences.

Fleeing to America, he met a great ornithologist called William Bartram, who re-kindled his interest in birds and taught him how to properly articulate himself with scientific terminology.

He spent 10 years travelling 10,000 miles, collecting and collating bird accounts and portraits, then publishing them. Their beauty to this day is unsurpassed.

He is regarded as the Father of American Ornithology.

Glossary/Explication

LINES 1–2 Robert Tannahill was a Paisley weaver and poet who suffered from terrible depression, thus committed suicide. See also James Coats (30).

LINES 3–4 'Youth o' yarns' – Alexander himself was also a weaver.

LINE 5 He was apprenticed to a weaver by Lochwinnoch's side, which may have given him his early interest in ornithology. He did much of his composing by the daunting Castle Semple. Lochwinnoch is now a bird sanctuary and visitor centre.

LINES 6–7 Herring being fished by the fish-hawk, or osprey, is an awesome sight.

LINE 8 From one of his own songs, called 'The Fisherman's Hymn'. The fish-hawk is another name for the osprey.

LINES 9–13 Although he had begun selling popular poetry, he used his talent to comment on what he saw as the unfair treatment of weavers by their employers, which resulted in him being jailed for libel. So his 'warp and woof' – same as 'warp and weft' on a loom – the threads or yarns being woven at right angles to each other – here means his tapestry of cunning words.

LINES 14–16 He emigrated to America in 1794, due to financial pressure.

LINES 17–18 At that time, he tried to teach on bird engravings, to the best of his ability.

LINES 19–26 Wilson came under the gentle tutelage of elder Bartram. Under the patriarch's guidance, he learned to draw, to describe and identify difficult birds, and to understand scientific literature honed from the Bartram library.

LINES 27–30 Exploring much of the eastern half of the USA, observing, drawing and selling his output, he travelled over 10,000 miles with 'Poll', a Carolina Parrot, for over 10 years, despite ill health and lack of funds.

LINES 31–34 His travels resulted in his nine-volume work, *American Ornithology*, published between 1808 and 1814.

LINES 35–36 He conducted the first breeding bird census in Bartram's Garden, correcting earlier errors of taxonomy, and publishing many observations of natural history.

LINES 37–38 His coloured plates are unsurpassed in beauty.

LINE 40 In America he is called the Father of American Ornithology.

ALEXANDER WILSON

Though Tannahill kent ways with weaving,
Yet heart and quill engaged in grieving,
Another youth o' yarns frae Paisley
Would love the loom o' bard-like phrases.
By Semple Castle's Loch, he'd write   5
Of herrings, and the osprey's flight.
On many trips, yon bard did wish her,
'God bless the fish-hawk and the fisher.'
With bold verse written he defamed
Employers in the weavers' trade.   10
His warp and woof a' words not woolly,
Brought on him suits that judged him cruelly.
Twixt jail and fines, which broke his back,
In sare a flight, his worn wings flapped,
In restless motion to reach over   15
The western ocean to teach bolder
To Pennsylvania's Kingsessing,
On etchings, sharing artful lessons.
When William Bartram met that gallant,
He kindled that man's better talents,   20
By bringing back his likes and loves
For wings which flapped in skies above.
Beneath that patriarch's fair hand,
He'd glean a greater knack tae grasp,
Identify, relate and draw,   25
In science-like terms, collate and call.
A parrot that he named as Poll,
From Carolina's native stock,
Espoused his side to cheer and cherish,
Ten thousand miles through east sae merry.   30
No time he'd lose relating, counting,
Through nine bird books collate, accounting.
He'd first collect three hundred pieces,
Then six and twenty further species,
Then he corrected errors charted,   35
And breeding census next he started.
His Blue Jay, Gold Finch and Spoonbill,
In plumaged portraits have soon thrilled,
Near all who saw those birds thereafter,
From ornithology's first father.   40

27 CHARLES MACINTOSH 1766–1843

Born in Glasgow, the son of a chemical manufacturer of Highland stock, Charles Macintosh mass produced cudbear, sal ammoniac and Prussian blue dyes for fabrics.

With some waste naphtha, and dissolving rubber using by-product coal-tar, Macintosh glued two pieces of cloth together, thus inventing the raincoat. This led to the development of the life jacket and the rubber airbed which was used on Sir John Franklin's Arctic expedition.

Here I have drawn on a comparison of the garb of the old Highlander, the belted-plaid based on a sett of one found on Culloden, reputed to have belonged to a Macintosh.

Glossary/Explication

LINES 1–6 The plaid referred to here is now in the Moy Hall collection and is thought to be part of a plaid belonging to one of the Macintoshes, found on Culloden Moor after the battle of 1746. The colours and intricacy of the sett indicate that it had belonged to a gentleman of high degree, since the red and blue on it would have been procured from imported, expensive cochineal beetle and indigo dyes respectively.

LINES 7–10 'In urban clime' – in this case, Glasgow. The Gaels then held a strong traditional legacy of cloth making. Glasgow still has a high population of Gaels.

LINES 13–14 Cudbear is purple or violet dyeing powder prepared from lichens, patented by Cuthbert Gordon who was an 18th century chemist.

LINES 15–20 He manufactured his own sal ammoniac and Prussian blue dye, and introduced lead and aluminium acetates. Alum was used as a mordant for fixing colours, which Charles made from ammonia, aluminium sulphate and potassium. He managed to get potassium by toasting seaweed which helped the Highland kelp industry (preceding the Clearances). He collected ammonia from stale human urine gathered from farmhouse pails.

LINES 21–30 – LINE 22 'Gas fitted' – see also William Murdoch (18). One of his waste products was naphtha (inflammable oil gained by dry distillation of organic substances, such as coal, shale or petroleum). He came up with the idea of producing a waterproof fabric made from two layers of cloth glued together with a solution of India rubber dissolved in naphtha. Such stiff cloth proved difficult to tailor, but never discouraged, and with the help of a scientist friend, he improved the technique of dissolving rubber using by-product coal tar to soften it.

LINES 31–32 In 1823 Macintosh patented this process, giving the garment its internationally renowned name.

LINES 33–36 Sir John Franklin's expedition to the Arctic in 1824, for which the world's first inflatable life jacket and rubber airbed were made. See also Sir John Ross (33) and Alexander Maconachie (36).

LINE 37 Charles linked up with a Manchester company in order to manufacture at a greater rate.

LINES 39–40 Adaptation of my nova-riddle for the raincoat.

CHARLES MACINTOSH

On Culloden's field was found a plaidie
In coloured tweeds all bound unfaded.
With red, green, blue, fine lines criss-crossing,
Of genteel hue with sides stitched, knotting,
From hardy cloth of tight combed yarn,   5
Of Macintosh's bright bold clan.
Of that brave race, another time,
A clan heir came in urban clime.
When olden wisdom did prevail,
From home spun wit o' thrifty Gael.   10
He'd rattle fro and to his shuttle,
With dye imported too sae subtle.
'Though grey's e'er gaunt or dull, maist don it,
Let's make Bert Gordon's cudbear profit,'
Said Charles, 'I'll tone that wool from lichens,   15
And sal ammoniac, blue for dyeing,
With alum mordent checking colours,
Potassium brought from kelp in burners,
And ammonia honed from urine stale,
Men folks do pour or put in pails.'   20
He'd take real stock, this steward sae thrifty,
When waste he saw from new gas fitted.
Said, 'Naphtha,' he, 'for bridge and cover,
Let's plaster weel with India rubber
Well jammed between two sides o' cloth,   25
No mad mean feast for mite nor moth.'
Yet pliable cloth this was not truly,
But liable not to thwart him throughly.
He softened o'er that screen resolving,
'By-product coal tar needs dissolving.'   30
All that guid lot did lay ne'er latent,
For Macintosh wid bear the patent.
A bed aerated for foul floors,
Would help the daring dawn outdoors,
And tough life jackets hard inflate,   35
For trudging tracks tae Arctic's gate.
The Macintosh is famed worldwide,
But backed and born on rainy Clyde.
When patter comes, it coddles close,
And flatters mums in model's pose.   40

Born at Cromdale in Speyside, James MacGrigor, the son of a merchant, studied medicine at Aberdeen, then joined the army as a surgeon.

He stood by the side of the Duke of Wellington as surgeon-general in the Peninsular Wars, at battles in the Pyrenees and Toulouse, and began revolutionalising the care of the wounded in the field at Vitoria. He was able to ensure that the wounded were treated in field hospitals, became fit again and returned to battle.

Although his career was over by the Battle of Waterloo, he was knighted and is regarded as being the founder of the Royal Army Medical Corps.

Glossary/Explication

LINES 1–2 Artists in Ireland have enjoyed tax exemption status since the 1920s.

LINES 2–4 In Phoenix Park, in the south of Dublin, stands Wellington's Statue, the tallest in Ireland. During the struggles for Irish independence in the early part of the 20th century, the newly formed Irish Republican Army destroyed Nelson's column with explosives in that town. However, Wellington's statue was left by them unharmed, because, according to tradition, Wellington's family had been of certain respected Anglo-Irish lairds who were not always at loggerheads with the native Irish.

LINES 5–9 Cromdale is in Strathspey, where James was the son of a self-made merchant who specialised in the making of stockings for military regiments.

LINES 10–14 He studied medicine at Aberdeen and Edinburgh Universities, then went south to make a fortune as a doctor in London before joining the army. The Connaught Rangers were an Irish regiment.

LINES 15–18 'Trod with treatment' – MacGrigor was the first to help the wounded back into service again. He was shipwrecked during his time in the West Indies. In Bombay and Ceylon, as superintending surgeon to the army, he had to deal with an outbreak of the plague and he himself suffered from malaria.

LINES 19–32 MacGrigor revolutionised the care of the wounded and was present in the battlefield in Vitoria (1813), the Pyrenees and Toulouse. He was able to ensure that the wounded were treated in field hospitals, and became fit again to return to the battlefield. Wellington said he could not have won Vitoria without him. This led to MacGrigor receiving his knighthood.

LINE 33 Chief Medical Officer for all of Britain.

LINE 35–39 'MacGrigor' is pronounced 'MacGreegor', from the proper Gaelic spelling and pronouncation of *MacGriogair*, i.e. MacGregor. His service was over by the time of the Battle of Waterloo. *The Scalpel and the Sword* is a book written by Lady Mary MacGrigor, a direct descendant of Sir James. She also wrote and co-produced much Clan Gregor history and beautiful pictorials with the present chief Sir Malcolm MacGregor of MacGregor.

LINE 40 Sir James MacGrigor is regarded as being the founder of the Royal Army Medical Corps.

SIR JAMES MacGRIGOR

In Dublin town where stars have stature,
On public ground there stands a statue,
Which yet on times of strife stayed standing,
Old Nelson's height of might made landings.
A young Gael, Wellington's same age,   5
On Cromdale entered world's great stage.
Though finest specimens of stockings,
For Highland regiments' worn walking,
His father seamed, this James did sever,
For Aberdeen the same did enter,   10
With urge to join the army as
A surgeon of the master class.
He fought all dangers through his corps
Of Connaught's Rangers during wars.
West Indies, Flanders, Bombay, Egypt   15
There injured rankers trod with treatment.
In battles, fevers, and ships wrecked,
He'd handle weel their hardy tests.
As General and soldier-surgeon,
The Peninsular Wars would urge him,   20
Through gore with gall to mind the maimed,
From Portugal through heights o' Spain.
In Toulouse and the Pyrenees,
This guru'd gladly bring relief.
And revolution he did surely   25
Affect for poorly weary wounded.
In hospitals, on fields, his men
Would foster will to wield again.
'We couldn't have,' his proud duke shouted,
'Vitoria without you! routed,   30
Your fine good work with talents merit,
A knighthood for this gallant service.'
This medical high chief in office
As veteran had sealed his promise.
MacGrigor's service was well through,   35
As hero vet, by Waterloo.
The Scalpel and the Sword, proclaim,
By clansmen after yon old name,
Of how this scion o' bravest breed,
Had founded the RAMC.   40

Born in Glasgow, Robert Stevenson was brought up by his step-father, and father-in-law to be, Thomas Smith. He was educated at Glasgow and Edinburgh universities.

He designed and built a large number of lighthouses, his most well known being the Bell Rock off the coast of Arbroath. He also improved their lighting systems by adding parabolic reflectors and intermittent lights.

His reputation for this achievement gained him contracts for building canals, roads, railways, bridges and statues.

He is the father of the great Stevenson lighthouse dynasty.

Glossary/Explication

LINES 1–4 The Bell Rock lighthouse, which was completed in the year 1811, stands on a semi-submerged reef out at sea. It is visible on a clear day from the seashore at Arbroath.

LINE 5–9 Robert Stevenson's father-in-law and stepfather were the same person. See Thomas Smith (16). LINE 7 – The first letters of each word read 's.o.s.s.o.s.' – the old mayday call, 'Save Our Souls'.

LINES 10–12 From 1797 to 1843 Robert Stevenson designed and built many lighthouses.

LINES 13–18 During winters, Robert continued his part-time education in Glasgow and Edinburgh Universities but in summer supervised the installation of lights on progressively more remote sites. His combination of theory and practice, along with his energy, carefulness and natural ability, also enabled him to undertake the design of lighthouses.

LINES 19–20 In 1808, he succeeded Smith as Chief Executive of the Northern Lighthouses Board.

LINES 25–30 During his career, he designed or constructed at least 25 Scottish lighthouses and improved Smith's reflectors with the addition of parabolic reflectors and more powerful lamps. He also introduced a system of intermittent and flashing lights to the lighthouses, to enable individual lights to be identified by mariners, and the mast lantern for lightships.

LINES 31–34 His successful involvement in the Bell Rock lighthouse brought him commissions for other civil engineering works. From 1812 until his retirement in 1846, he established the firm's reputation in Scotland and Northern England for designing improvements listed in the verses. LINES 33–34 Malleable iron, instead of cast-iron rails, for railways.

LINE 36–40 In 1822, under Robert's direction, the iron jib crane used on the Bell Rock lighthouse lifted the twice as large-as-life statue of the late Viscount Melville to the top of a slender 41 m high column in St Andrew Square, Edinburgh.

ROBERT STEVENSON

The Bell Rock stands still, still highlighting
A bedrock brand in skills far sighted,
In wettest wilds of cold hard coasts,
Eleven miles from old Arbroath.
A Scottish wit, this laddie's mentor,   5
Was Thomas Smith, the lamp inventor.
That sage of saving souls on seas,
Would wage on waves his wars for weeks.
Whose stepson Robert, in all stations,
Would set up stockade installations,   10
Much more and more, on more remote
Rough coastal cold blown shores exposed.
In Glesga' toon and in Auld Reekie,
He'd settle doon for winter reading,
Where theories practised with enhancement,   15
Might cheer the artist with enchantment.
Refined reflector lamps bright, mounted,
Designed he next for high lighthouses.
Preparing coastal rigs yet farther,
He'd take the post of his stepfather,   20
When off the east coast he'd start raising
Bell Rock in fierce cold seas a-raging,
That made his greatest contribution,
And name sae famous for volution,
For five and twenty towers sae fine,   25
Designed with plenty power tae shine,
By adding on first, through each sector,
His parabolic new reflectors,
And intermittent flashing lights,
Far did distinguish craft with site.   30
Canals, paths, channels, roads with routings,
And grandest harbours, coasts improving,
He pioneered with railway trails
Of pliable, veering, varied rails.
Great bridges this guid Brainheart built,   35
And shifting jib-like crane that thirled
And hoisted up the Viscount Melville,
To join him trussed at sky bound levels,
Right out, right from grey land to stare,
Lighthouse-like, o'er St Andrew Square.   40

30 JAMES COATS 1774–1857

James Coats was born in Paisley into a family of weavers.

After serving his apprenticeship as a weaver, he spent six years in the army but returned home to the weaving trade. He found a niche in the market for Canton Crepe, which, as opposed to being imported from China, could be produced domestically.

With the collaboration of other manufacturers, he built a firm in Paisley which was further developed by his three sons after him. Canton Crepe and cotton thread were their legacy of worldwide renown, as might be seen yet on the colourful Coats' Brocades.

Glossary/Explication

LINES 1–8 The Paisley weavers, apart from being great artisans in their own right, were also renowned political activists. See Alexander Wilson (26).

LINES 9–10 The Paisley Shawl is an elaborate pattern based on Hindu and Arabic motifs.

LINES 11–12 The River Leine runs through Hanover in Lower Saxony, hence 'the Leine King's shilling'.

LINES 13–14 He joined the Ayrshire Fencibles, a cavalry regiment, then came back home to the weaving trade. See also note on LINES 9–13 on Alexander Wilson (26).

LINES 15–16 This is where he returned to his trade in Paisley and got married.

LINES 17–30 Seeing a market for Canton Crepe, the majority of which at that time was imported from China, he set out to produce this material in his own factory. Canton Crepe was made from silk, the manufacture of which had been introduced to Paisley in 1760 by Humphrey Fulton; hence both the raw material and the skilled labour were readily available. Another manufacturer, James Whyte, was also trying to produce it. He and Coats combined their skills in partnership, producing Canton Crepe into quantities enough to corner the market.

LINES 31–34 As his fortunes increased, Coats built a house in Back Row, Ferguslie, Paisley and became sleeping partner with Ross and Duncan, thread twisters, acquiring knowledge of the business of the production of Canton Crepe which requires yarn with a particular twist. When his contract with them expired, he built a small mill at Ferguslie, producing his own thread, using a 12 HP engine. This mill was the forerunner of the JP Coats site.

LINES 35–36 On retirement in 1830, his three erudite sons – Peter in merchandising, James in manufacturing and Thomas in engineering – managed the business. The company expanded rapidly during the 1830s, both at home and overseas, and by 1840, three quarters of their trade was in the USA.

LINES 37–40 'Shewn sae neat' – sewn so neat (Scots). Between 1934 and 1939 the company sponsored the Needlework Development in Scotland scheme, a collaboration between art and design education and industry. The scheme encouraged needlework and therefore the sale of JP Coats thread. Coats' Needlework in Scotland Development Scheme embroidery can still be seen on display in schools in Scotland.

JAMES COATS

Auld Paisley town's ain working weavers
Did bravely spout sare words sae eager.
For sake of fair-play's wage, their part
Compared yon trade wi' ancient craft.
James Coats was raised in that town yearning   5
To hone his trade with background learning,
His shuttle always clicked-clacked-clicking,
While thrusting forward kicks, back kicking.
It was the Paisley Shawl sae seemly
Adorned and draped that donned sae dreamily   10
But James did break frae minding milling,
Tac claim or take the Leine King's shilling
On horse with sword tae served six years,
Then call o' warp and weft wid hear,
Tae twist sae fine threads twirled in plaidies,   15
And intertwine next with his lady.
Identifying far-fetched parts,
He then did spy this market gap:
'Since folks worldwide wear Canton Crepe,'
Said Coats, 'I might mare mark-up make.   20
Since crepe is mostly brought from China,
Let's save importing costs for finer
And skilful means to out wit markets,
By thrift in reaping our silk harvest,
For Fulton makes this finest fibre   25
Wi' tools o' trade tae twine-twist tighter.
I'll bond with Whyte, no more to loiter,
For from this side, the globe's oor oyster.'
For world's main mart those partners made,
Their first fair brand o' Canton Crepe.   30
James then did take to crepe twill twisting,
At Ferguslie's new thread-mill building,
Where 12 HP did push production,
At better speed on spools for function,
Which has yet in the US led,   35
The market as its purest thread.
Yet o'er in Scottish schools they'll see,
James Coats type brocades shewn sae neat,
Whose own good firm did start as norm,
Those sewn pure gifts as an art form.   40

From Dundee, James Keiller, a merchant in that town, was no stranger to importing.

One day he went to collect a delivery from a ship, only to discover that he had received, in error, bitter oranges from the continent. Rather than waste them, his wife, Janet, came up with the idea of making a new brand of jam as an aid for morning digestion.

With the help of her husband and his nephew, they developed quickly into a company to mass produce marmalade for a worldwide market.

Although they became world class confectioners, marmalade is what they are best known for.

Glossary/Explication

LINES 1–4 Before the Union of the Crowns in 1603, Scots were a healthier, more virile race than they are now, and were more multi-lingual and European orientated. We ate many of the same foods as the French, who were our major trading and military partners. We also traded with many other countries in Europe on our own terms.

LINES 5–8 Mary Queen of Scots is reputed to have eaten a solid sugary jelly of marmelos – quinces imported from Portugal as 'marmelada'. She took this for her own health. 'Marie Malade': Mary's Malady (French), hence 'marmalade', from 'Marmelade pour Marie malade'.

LINES 9–10 The long decline of healthy food sources between 1603 and 1707, with the ultimate exile of our native monarchs, was to leave us with a long legacy of malnutrition.

LINES 11–16 James Keiller, a well-established merchant in Dundee, whilst checking a shipment delivery, mistakenly bought a consignment of bitter Seville oranges from a ship which had just come into port.

LINES 17–28 But necessity or opportunity being the mother of invention, his wife Janet (though some say her name was Margaret) went about making the oranges into a jelly not dissimilar to quince jelly. However, most early French marmalades were pulped to a puree. But Janet was acquainted with a French recipe, which would include cutting the peel into chips. This thrifty lady also noticed that marmalade, not being as dense as puree, would take less time to cook. With the use of the bitter oranges, she changed marmalade into being an aid for morning digestion.

LINES 29–38 When James realised that his wife had come up with a very marketable commodity, he set up a company to produce marmalade. His very own nephew, called Wedderspoon Keiller, was also involved in what was clearly their family business, so he invented a machine to cut peel for mass production. By the mid-1870s Keillers of Dundee's very own marmalade became popular at breakfast-time tables all over the world. They became one of the world's largest confectioners and were one of the first companies to gain a registered trademark.

LINES 39–40 The adapted last two lines of the nova-riddle for marmalade.

JANET AND JAMES KEILLER

In golden days gone, folks have claimed,
Our olden gates or doors of trade,
Brought dear delights from bigger states,
To feast the sight or tickle tastes.
When clear hard jam did help Queen Mary   5
Maire Malade! the French cheered gaily,
The Portuguese did bring and sell,
From over seas this quince-like jell.
Though dynasties and times departed,
Folk did yet crave class finer fancies.   10
A Dundee merchant and main dealer
That work-peers kent and ca'ed James Keiller,
One day while sifting, checking shipments,
Did stray near mid-ship's deck and tripped when
His pack he saw all wrongly filled   15
With tart keen oranges from Seville.
This exercise which James did spurn,
To enterprise his lady turned.
Thought Janet, 'Yes! Just like quince jelly.
Let's have it French in style mixed, maybe?   20
For prudence sake, not bulky, thickly,
Like puree, paste all pulped sae pickly,
But stringed wi' thin chipped peels of orange
Sae sticky, sitting steeped like porridge.'
Through all her skills, this gem sae thrifty,   25
Cured morning ills wi' gel sae prickly.
Called marmalade, to edge ingestion,
And farther aid for best digestion.
A business pact her man built up,
To gift in jars and pack the stuff.   30
His brother's son helped him to start it,
Lift up, then run, then hit new markets,
By craft, procuring guid bold yields,
Through mass producing chips o' peel.
On breakfast trays and shops, I'm told,   35
This steadfast tasty pot o' gold,
And innovation borne by Janet
Has thrilled most nations o'er the planet.
From fair Dundee on toast for aye,
Its taste appeals for folks tae buy.   40

32 ALEXANDER CUMMING C.1732–1814

Born in Edinburgh, Alexander Cumming became a clock- and watch-maker there, but moved to London to continue his trade.

Envisioning a world beyond the grasp of his contemporaries, Alexander developed and finally invented a water closet with the Strap. Based on older ideas, this was a sliding valve between the bowl and the trap. In other words, it could be flushed at the pull of a lever.

He patented this in London in 1775. His invention very quickly caught on.

Here I have played on the term water closet with the London postal code West Central, both being WC.

Glossary/Explication

LINES 1–6 Most of the original toilet bowls were white. Those functions of nature remind us starkly of our equality.

LINES 7–10 This is not an appointment to be postponed.

LINES 11–16 Watch- and clock-maker was his first occupation.

LINES 17–24 Cumming believed that there was a better way to answer the call of nature than by using chamber pots and open trenches so he invented the Strap, which was a sliding valve between the bowl and the trap. It was the first of its kind, which he patented in 1775. However, it did not take long before others followed Cumming's lead: two years later Samuel Prosser applied and received a patient for a plunger closet.

LINES 25–32 The letters WC are almost as universally recognised as 'hello' or 'bank', etc. Almost every type of edifice now has an inside toilet. LINE 30 – 'Howff' – favourite haunt or meeting place, often a public house (Scots).

LINES 33–36 Again, as we see in LINES 7–10 above, waiting time for the use of the WC can be lengthy, but would prove to be a better alternative than witnessing the waste being thrown out of the windows at a certain time of the evening, as happened in old Edinburgh, where the French phrase *regardez l'eau!* was exclaimed as a warning to any passers-by. This might be one of the explanations for the term 'Auld Reekie' for Edinburgh. The last syllable of *regardez l'eau* is pronounced as 'loo', from which we get the same term colloquially for toilet or WC.

LINE 39 Until fairly recently, tolls for the use of the WC were paid for by putting a penny (in the old currency) through a small slot on the WC's door, where the penny dropped or clunked in order to gain access.

ALEXANDER CUMMING

This bright great throne placed like a folly,
And white bare cone makes life so jolly,
By sitting, really quietly in it,
Whilst lifting grief in five wee minutes,
Is deemed as wise in all proud places,   5
As equaliser of our races.
'Tis quite a race against the time,
To find that place, in every clime.
When nature cries you've got to go
To make your tryst with yon commode.   10
But time to keep to, day to day,
Is dire a need, for maist to gauge.
Auld Reekie raised, for making watches,
Complete with chains to place in pockets,
This Cumming lad betook the summon,   15
And cunning craft resumed in London,
But had his aim or careful planning,
For sanitation's care re-panning,
By flushing foul waste so offensive,
Fast gushing out made more effective.   20
His sliding valve, with thong fixed on it,
Besides its trap – the water closet,
Would change domestic sanitation,
As ways for cleansing in all nations.
West Central's postcode in that town's   25
First letters boast more and abound
On doors all o'er the earth in plenty,
Where folks for tolls need spend a penny.
In hospital, hotel, bank, house,
In shopping mall, motel, mart, howff,   30
In train or airport, school or college,
It caters fair from youth to auld age.
That grief for freeing, all will find,
A wee convenience of this kind,
With lengthy stand in landing queue,   35
Is better than *regardez l'eau*!
That caring kindly slothless Scot,
Did take the time to plot this pot,
For sum or fee to clunk in quickly,
On wcs in London City.   40

33 SIR JOHN ROSS 1777–1856

Born in Wigtownshire, son of a minister, John Ross joined the Royal Navy at the age of nine, rising to captain very quickly and then commander, leading a Swedish fleet.

This successful officer led an expedition in 1818 to find a route by sea through the Northwest Passage, which Alexander Mackenzie had pioneered by stream and on foot in 1793. John's first mission was not particularly successful but a second mission brought about the discovery of the Boothia Gulf and Peninsula, and King William Island.

His nephew, James Clark Ross, then discovered the Magnetic North Pole.

Glossary/Explication

LINES 1–4 The parish of Inch in Wigtownshire. His father was Rev Andrew Ross.

LINES 5–6 He was nine years old when he entered the navy and served in the Napoleonic Wars.

LINES 7–14 For almost 30 years he was to navigate without interruption. He was first to serve in the Mediterranean Ocean, then afterwards in the English Channel. Rising to the rank of captain, he would later command a Swedish fleet.

LINES 15–22 He was very successful as an officer, which is why he was chosen by the Admiralty to command the 1818 Arctic expedition, when led by sea in search of the Northwest Passage, which would link the Atlantic and Pacific Oceans. In 1793, Honest Alex, (Alexander Mackenzie (24)) found the first route to the Northwest Passage through rivers, streams and tracks, but the route was too rough to be used commercially at that time. See also LINE 33. John concluded that Lancaster Sound was enclosed by mountains and thus provided no western outlet.

LINES 23–30 On this second voyage, Ross was accompanied by his nephew, James Clark Ross. It was during this expedition that the younger Ross discovered the magnetic North Pole. The expedition was also notable for the discovery of Boothia Peninsula and Gulf, which he named after the voyager's sponsor, Felix Booth, as well as King William Island. In recognition for his discoveries, John was given gold medals from the English, French and Swedish geographical societies, including the Pole Star, Sweden and a CB with a knighthood. LINE 24 – *Breenge* – to rush forward recklessly (Scots).

LINES 31–34 John Franklin – British Arctic explorer and Tasmanian governor who attempted an expedition to the Northwest Passage in 1847 but perished in the effort with his crew. See also Charles Macintosh (27), notes on LINES 33–36 and Alexander Maconochie (36), notes on LINES 17–24.

LINES 35–40 Between himself and his nephew, he discovered the Magnetic North Pole, but it was his nephew who would make the same attempt for the South Pole and discovered Antarctic for Queen Victoria. See also James Clerk Ross (45).

SIR JOHN ROSS

Old Wigtown's green and rolling parish
Called Inch, did see a hopeful marriage,
And raise with zest a cleric's child,
In nature's restful western wilds.
Sae brave and early on adventures,   5
The naval service John did enter,
Whilst viewing all 'twix all her stations,
And cruising, logging observations.
Around the Med this lad well served,
Then round the English Channel swerved,   10
Up rose so quickly with promotion,
And hosts of ships led in cold oceans,
For Sweden's fleet as acting captain,
Then even reached high rank commanding.
Six years he served on postings fair,   15
Whilst seeking yet for bolder dares,
For this true sailor's next guid mission
Was rigged to make an expedition
To Northwest Passage through wild seas,
Which honest Alex took by streams.   20
They'd find near naethin' which seemed new,
But five years later did renew
Another sea jaunt in yon sphere,
To further breenge on this frontier.
With sore researching, four years forward,   25
His core success did score real honours:
The English, French and Swedes all settled,
On this guid helmsman three gold medals.
Twix Pole Star Sweden, gift for mighthood,
At home a CB, with a knighthood.   30
Another voyage did Ross start in,
To rummage for aged Sir John Franklin.
Who claimed an entry gained by sea,
That A. Mackenzie made by feet,
Another one Ross of his wit,   35
John's brother's son was on this trip,
Who aye did form new roles effective,
In finding north's true pole magnetic.
Though great acclaim Sir John achieved,
Much claim to fame this Ross would yield.   40

Born in Glasgow, Andrew Ure was to be a multiple genius as a scriptural geologist, surgeon, medical doctor, Professor of Natural Philosophy, and first ever consultant chemist. Doing analysis for the Board of Customs, he exposed large-scale criminal activity. He established an observatory in Glasgow and was appointed astronomer. There he designed and made a 14 ft reflecting telescope.

He was one of the Honorary Fellows of the Geographical Society of London and the Astronomical Society, and became a Fellow of the Royal Society.

His journals included metrology, and latent heat. He was a linguist, classical and biblical scholar. He also invented thermostatic control.

Glossary/Explication

LINES 1–4 In the Bible, Genesis 1:2, the word 'was' in other places of that chapter translates 'became', which, through other related scripture of the same topic, refers to Lucifer's fall from Heaven. Although he had originally been God's light bearer, he became the bringer of darkness. He first reveals himself as 'the Serpent' for his cunning ways and subtlety, in Genesis 3.

LINES 5–13 Many Biblical scholars at that time erroneously concluded that since Adam lived about 6,000 years ago that the Earth must be the same age. Noah is recorded in Genesis 6, but the Ice Age did not come as a result of his flood, rather from whence 'darkness fell upon the face of the deep'.

LINES 14–24 He studied first at Glasgow then at Edinburgh, obtaining an MA in 1798–99 and his MD in Glasgow in 1800, serving briefly as an army surgeon before settling in Glasgow. In 1804 he became Professor of Natural Philosophy at the Andersonian Institute, giving lectures on chemistry and mechanics. In 1830 he resigned, moved to London and became the first consultant chemist in Britain. By 1834 he was doing analysis for the Board of Customs. He risked a lot of friendships for the sake of scientific truth in exposing large-scale criminal activity. In 1908 he helped to establish the Glasgow Observatory and was appointed its astronomer. The famous astronomer William Herschel helped him to install a 14 ft reflecting telescope, which Ure had designed and manufactured.

LINES 25–30 He wrote seven books and more than 53 scientific journal articles. Many dealt with chemical problems but others dealt with gravity.

LINES 31–32 A paper in 1817 on latent vapours was influential in the development of many modern meteorological theories.

LINES 33–36 For cotton mills' vats to regulate temperature for dyeing in order to produce an even product, Ure patented the bi-metal thermostat in 1830.

LINES 36–40 He was also a linguist, classical scholar of foreign literature, and had read deeply in theology and Biblical criticism. All in all, he was 'one of those brilliantly versatile men of science' in the 19th century, who, according to his contemporaries, had an 'encyclopedic understanding'.

ANDREW URE

When Lucifer from Heaven fell,
To choose his bed of earth as hell,
And darkness on the face o' deep,
He masked his sordid gaze for keeps.
Few yet hae learned nor yet hae fathomed,   5
That earth was there long e'er came Adam,
And those affairs e'er shook this place,
Before there came a human race.
This was unknown in ears coeval,
Who thought the globe appeared more peopled,   10
And said the ice did cover over
The earth, in times the flood of Noah.
Although he followed what was taught,
This worthy doctor brought a lot,
By paving patterns to align,   15
And make what mattered for mankind.
As first consultant chemist ever,
His gifts resultant well endeavoured
To bring to light so rife and raging,
His guid insight to crime far-ranging.   20
His sky-hole saw in darkened Glasgow
His spy-scope for the stars that sparkle,
Which though designed and built as special,
Was more aligned by William Herschel.
He left his dealings laid in journals,   25
Of dwelling heating, weightless tumbles,
Gun-powder, matches, detonation,
Heat power matched with ventilation,
With thunder-rods, heat latent issues,
And studies on decaying tissues.   30
His well forecasted weather views,
With thermostatic check he'd prove,
Whilst copyrighting all honed skills,
For cloth with dyes for cotton mills.
His pet bi-metal thermostat,   35
Would set and settle temp o' vat.
This linguist and a man distinguished
In scriptures, classics and guid English,
Held high hopes clearly aye demanding
Encyclopedic understanding.   40

35 SIR DAVID BREWSTER 1781–1868

Born in Jedburgh, with a very disciplined upbringing, David
Brewster would become a multiple inventor.

  Although he started out as a journalist, he was fascinated with
light and crystallography, and would become known for the law
of polarisation of biaxial crystals.

  He invented new types of micrometer and the dioptric lens as
well as new types of microscopes, including the wrongly-attrib-
uted Coddington Lens.

  He invented the kaleidoscope but his patent was not fool-proof.
However he did patent his next device, the stereoscope, which
caught Queen Victoria's attention and custom, causing it to flood
the market.

Glossary/Explication

LINES 1–4 He was a writer, scientist, university principal and a member of the British
Association for the Advancement of Science, and a multiple inventor.

LINES 5–12 He was from Jedburgh. His school-master father was a strict disciplinarian
and wanted David and his three brothers to be church clerics, but David's interest in
the Church diminished and he became a journalist and editor in Edinburgh.

LINES 13–16 Optical instrumentation and the theory of light would be his main passion
and the law of polarisation of biaxial crystals is what he would become best known for.
This would even bear his name, which would be associated with founding crystallog-
raphy and experimental optics. He invented the kaleidoscope.

LINES 17–20 A version of the nova-riddle for the kaleidoscope.

LINES 21–22 He tried to patent this in 1814 but because the patent was incomplete,
another instrument maker began to copy it.

LINE 23–24 'Was no mummer' – actor (Scots). His microscopes included the Coddington
Lens, which was named after Henry Coddington, a Cambridge tutor who made its use
public in 1829, nine years after Brewster had invented it.

LINES 25–28 He invented several types of micrometer for the dioptric lens, making
lighthouse lamps more effective. See also Thomas Smith (16) and Robert Stevenson
(29).

LINES 29–30 Said to be the first photographs with some colour.

LINES 31–34 He attempted to reform the university's administration at St Andrews
University. He afterwards went on to Edinburgh, where he became principal.

LINE 33 'BA Science's founding', i.e. the British Association of Advanced Science.

LINES 35–38 He designed a stereoscopic viewer and camera. The viewer looked into
two similar photo-slides side by side through two lenses and the images converged making
the image three dimensional. Through this scope, people could view everything from
exotic eastern monoliths to fine, historical European buildings. At the Great Exhibition
of 1851, Queen Victoria highly approved of and purchased one of them, resulting in
good public relations and a landslide in sales, so much so that within half a century,
one million were sold.

LINES 39–40 He was knighted not just for the stereoscope but for his scientific achieve-
ment generally.

SIR DAVID BREWSTER

Let's chart a list of such a man
That passes fist tae upper arm,
Of findings, light refined inventions,
Combined with quite benign intentions.
Down south east's side of this old nation,   5
With sound delight for innovation,
With drilling firmly made at hame,
Strict discipline did David gain.
His father oft as schooling master,
Would rap his rod with ruling ardour.   10
His son disdained the pastor's gown,
Which must have made his father frown.
But light he'd prove by facts not fickle,
Through brightly cool biaxial crystals.
That light o' hope would be his passion,   15
Kaleidoscope to be its fashion.
Like merry dancers tight and trim,
Who' set, advance inside the rim,
You'd come and glimpse gems' jolly spins,
Dance through a circus thronged yet thin.   20
Though business ever blazed sae blatant,
For this, he never paid the patent.
Yet high o' hope, he wis nae mummer,
For microscopes he'd fit tae further.
Micrometer on nights for lighthouse,   25
Dioptric lens of might to shine out,
Poor souls would reach with beaming beacons,
From shore or beach in fierce winds' seasons.
Light's core he'd craft re-mixed for others
On photographs he'd click all coloured.   30
In Fife he'd nearly change the norm,
Then ride to Reekie where reform
Would start with BA Science's founding,
To mak' this real alliance astounding
His scope to spy set pictures doubled,   35
Restored Her Highness in her troubles,
Which virtual three-D amused
A million, and the Queen who'd choose
To give a knighthood to this man,
Whose skill and sight would prove his plan.   40

Born in Leith, Alexander Maconochie joined the Royal Navy and travelled much but was captured and imprisoned for five years, never to forget the experience.

After being released, he rose to the rank of captain. His travels instilled within him an interest in the world's cultures and customs, so he taught geography in London.

After this he was employed in Tasmania penal colony and witnessed much cruelty there, where his moral conscience caused his dismissal. He was made governor of Norfolk Island and was the first man to introduce humane prison reform.

His compassion cost him his career there.

Glossary/Explication

LINES 1–10 He enlisted in the Royal Navy, becoming a prisoner of the Dutch, which would give him first-hand experience of captivity.

LINES 11–16 Although he rose to the rank of captain after being released from prison, his interest in geography, and the ways of the peoples of the world, took him to London, where he became secretary to the Royal Geographical Society and Professor of Geography at the University of London. He maintained an interest in the pacific region and from 1836 worked in Australia.

LINES 17–24 In 1836, with Sir John Franklin, who was to become the new Governor of the penal colony of Tasmania, Alexander moved to become his private secretary. He was utterly appalled by the brutal treatment that convicts received there. He witnessed them being manacled, mangled, flogged and savaged by dogs. He understood their plight and had compassion for them. This man with a moral conscience campaigned for reform, which upset the colonists who exploited the cheap labour of those poor, unfortunate people. He sent letters home highlighting those things and Franklin, being affronted at this, had Alexander dismissed. See also Charles Macintosh (27) notes on LINES 33–36, and Sir John Ross (33).

LINES 27–36 In 1840 he was appointed Superintendent of the penal settlement at Norfolk Island, 1,000 miles off the Australian coast, where inmates were sent from Tasmania for longer sentences. It is in this role that he is best remembered. He found the prison to be a brutal and miserable establishment and at once he began applying reforms to build a more humane environment. He put a stop to all punishments and replaced them with rewards for good behaviour. He improved conditions in the cells, and instituted a system whereby prisoners, through motivation, could shorten their sentences. This was similar to that of Lachlan MacQuarrie's reward system for good behaviour. See also Lachlan MacQuarrie (22). He released all convicts for a day on the Queen's birthday with privileges such as rum and fireworks, and all returned to him, proving that his humane method worked.

LINES 37–40 The Anglo authorities did not appreciate his methods and he was replaced in 1844. The prison quickly degenerated back into a regime of cruelty and recrimination. See Lachlan MacQuarrie (22).

ALEXANDER MACONOCHIE

A lad from Leith for sea insisted
And bad folks leave, to leave enlisted,
On naval roles, enrolled to rove
From cape or coast the whole world o'er.
Events did curb his standing stature,   5
Just when the Dutch this man did capture.
Five years in jail he'd lay there rotten
With tears, in pains, in prayers often,
To ne'er forget those fowl affronts,
Where seconds stretched frae hours tae months.   10
Yet on repeal he'd ply the capstan,
Ne'er long to lead then rise to captain.
But ways and wisdom of the world,
Would make his mission flag unfurl,
To summon knowledge proof with flair,   15
At London's college to declare.
But to Tasmania Alex crossed,
Where brute mad mania Franklin caused.
In savage stations causing conflict,
And castigation for the convicts,   20
Whose misdemeanours brought due anguish,
By living lean in lots to languish.
This man did see them torn by dogs,
Ripped, mangled, beaten, drawn and flogged,
So for reform oft long he'd press.   25
But lost his job, which caused real stress,
So Norfolk Island's lot he'd take,
Where all inside had longer stays.
There he improved their unsafe cells,
And eased the poorly inmates' hell.   30
With terms severe inside tae shorten,
They earned reprieve of time fair gotten.
The jailer's keys did turn the locks with
A day's release with rum and rockets.
His plan did prove, with kind persuasion,   35
That captives loosed, decline evasion.
But Anglo-rulers did insist,
Like Lachie too, he be dismissed.
This gentleman so goodly, gallant,
Had bettered standards, truth and balance.   40

Born in Jedburgh, Mary Fairfax, through little initial schooling, took up writing and by accident took an interest in algebra.

She then married a cousin but continued her work. When he died, he left her a comfortable legacy allowing her to continue working freely.

She married again, this time to another cousin, called Dr William Somerville. She produced many papers throughout her long life, including the 'Mechanisms of the Heavens'.

A member of the Royal Society, she was also the first woman elected to the Royal Astronomical Society. An Oxford College is named after her.

Glossary/Explication

LINES 1–6 Adaptation of her own words, 'Allowed to grow up a wild creature'. Mary's determination in the face of great adversity would be a beacon for women's equality. Despite her family's fortunate economic standing, Mary's education was, in her own words, 'scant and haphazard'. Her father was a vice admiral in the British Navy and was often away at sea. Her mother put few restraints on her, other than insisting that she learn to read the Bible and say her prayers.

LINES 7–12 She first studied arithmetic at the age of 13, at which time she, quite by accident, began to study algebra as she happened upon some mysterious symbols in the puzzles of a women's fashion magazine. And so began her quest.

LINES 13–16 Captain Samuel Greig, member of the Russian Navy, her first husband and cousin, had little interest in Mary's work. He died young.

LINES 17–20 Mary, now free to study, mastered J. Ferguson's Astronomy and became a student of Isaac Newton's *Principia*. She corresponded frequently with Scotsman William Wallace, mathematics master at the military college, on whose advice Mary accessed a small mathematics library.

LINES 21–24 She remarried in 1812 to another cousin, Dr William Somerville who, unlike her family, was very supportive of her work.

LINES 27–30 In 1826 she presented her paper, entitled *The Magnetic Properties of the Violet Rays of the Solar Spectrum* to the Royal Society. The paper was favourable and was joint first paper by a woman to be read to the Royal Society (published in its *Philosophical Transactions*).

LINES 31–34 Lord Brougham, pronounced 'Broo'am' was of the Society for the Diffusion of Useful Knowledge (SDUK). He asked Mary to write a popularised rendition of Laplace's *Mecanique Celeste* and Newton's *Principia*. The project was undertaken in secrecy and became *The Mechanism of the Heavens*, her greatest work.

LINES 35–36 Amongst her other works were *The Connection of the Physical Sciences*, *Physical Geography* and *Molecular and Microscopic Science*. She was elected to the Royal Astronomical Society in 1835, the first woman to receive such an honour.

LINES 37–38 In recognition of her, a portrait bust was commissioned by admirers in the Royal Society and placed in their great hall. It is now in the headquarters of the Society of London.

LINES 39–40 Somerville College, Oxford.

MARY FAIRFAX SOMERVILLE

Allowed to grow sae wild a creature,
And bound to boldly fight and feature
In generating terms to tender,
To venerate her gentler gender,
Was Mary's fate tae hack and hazard   5
Wha came fae training, 'scant, haphazard'.
Her learning short or ne'er exciting
Would never halt nor quell her writing.
A fashion magazine with symbols,
A passion far unleashed and kindled   10
With rapid start, for her to study
In algebra's codes in a hurry.
Her hubby, e'er not home it seemed,
Her studies held in low esteem.
His short life bade unfettered action,   15
Which brought bright Mary benefaction.
J. Ferguson's with Newton's truths,
Rare precious contributions could
With mathematics, gain her ground,
Attaching tactics, sane with sound.   20
Despite displeasure from her folks,
A kinder, gentler offer flowed.
A fun e'er filled good hearted man
Called Somerville, would have her hand.
Now, our wee nation's sacred rights   25
Empower each wave and age with might!
For esoteric terms magnetic
From rays o' spectrum's spell majestic's
Equation, Mary aye sae human,
First placed on paper, as a woman.   30
Lord Brougham sought her service next,
Which proved an awkward, nervy test,
Which then too risky was to mention,
Called *Mechanisms of the Heavens*.
She past mair tests with proofs sae clever   35
As RAS first woman ever.
A bust there surely indicated
Their trust was truly vindicated.
Her gall with knowledge does still claim
An Oxford college of her name.   40

38 JAMES CHALMERS 1782–1853

From Arbroath, James Chalmers was reared in the then thriving weaving trade.

He became a bookseller and publisher in Dundee. Perceiving a need for a more efficient postal service that people could afford, by 1834 he had already produced the first adhesive postage stamp, the idea being that people could pay the postage before it would be sent.

He lobbied Parliament who procrastinated, while three years later Roland Hill took the credit for it, being knighted as a result, and is entombed in Westminster Abbey.

A plaque in Dundee marks the spot where the real innovator had his shop.

Glossary/Explication

LINES 1–6 Roland Hill was accredited and knighted for the invention of the adhesive postage stamp three years after James Chalmers proposed it to parliament. There is a stone in Westminster that marks Hill's tomb. Here I have drawn on the comparison between Hill's grave and the Stone of Destiny, or Stone of Scone, which was stolen by Edward 1 of England (Longshanks) and taken to Westminster Abbey in the year 1296. It was retrieved by students who were active Scottish Nationalists in 1950 and returned to Scotland in 1997. See also David Douglas (43), notes on LINES 1–6.

LINES 7–10 James Chalmers was a weaver to trade, jute and cloth for sails probably being the main product.

LINES 11–14 He moved to Dundee where he became a bookseller, newspaper publisher and printer.

LINES 17–20 Post-runners delivered mail in the mountainous and remote areas. Before the coming of the military roads built by General George Wade in the 18th century, there were virtually no roads or bridges in the Highlands, therefore runners delivered the post over rough tracks or moorland.

LINES 21–24 If they could afford to, people would have to pay the postage on receipt, but many could not.

LINES 25–32 At this period in history, those receiving the letters paid for the postage if they could afford to do so, rather than the sender, losing income for the Post Office. The 'Penny Black' was the name of the first adhesive postage stamp, which was a square with the caption 'General Postage – Not exceeding half an ounce – One Penny' surrounded in an ornamented frame. His proposals for reform would include the now universally used system of using different colours of stamp for different rates of postage. Chalmers first produced an adhesive stamp in 1834, whereas Hill first proposed it in 1837. Parliament approved the plans in 1839.

LINES 33–36 A version of my nova-riddle for the postage stamp, i.e. it sits in the corner of the envelope but travels worldwide.

LINE 40 Chalmers's granddaughter erected a plaque stating 'originator of the adhesive postage stamp' on the site of his bookseller's shop in Dundee.

JAMES CHALMERS

Westminster Abbey's pilfered claim
Exhibits starkly chipped in stane,
Though not in granite Longshanks lifted,
Which honest sanguine Scots have shifted,
But on a tomb which lures a-looming,   5
With honours tooled, so soon assuming.
But at the coastal town, Arbroath,
A man would boast or frown at both.
For webs he'd weave with yarns by kicking,
Whilst there conceiving stamps for sticking.   10
So in Dundee where dreams could dwell,
This witty weaver reams would sell
Of papers, pamphlets, books, gifts, news,
To cater and amuse with views
And then insist that low-paid letters,   15
Would serve the inland post trade better.
A far cry was it when foot-runners,
Aye ran by lochs and glens through summers,
But roughed the rain through wind, cold hail
By trudging trails to bring folks mail.   20
Though post was freely mailed with storage,
Folks on receipt did pay the postage,
Which was sae weighty for the poor,
Which cost they'd hae tae oft procure.
'Reverse this state we will,' said Chalmers,   25
'Wee sepid-squares we'll tint as markers,
For ease in stating those rates boasted,
Where people pay before mail's posted.'
Said Parliament, 'We're for reform!',
Then Chalmers sent these proffers for   30
A stamp that these sealed letters lacked:
The artful neat wee Penny Black.
In corners sits it nightly, daily,
And on its niche sits tightly, sparely.
Far o'er the globe well well it rambles,   35
Yet from its home ne'er ne'er it ambles.
For all his innovative pains,
Another his ovation gained.
Although an honour Chalmers lacked,
An old shop corner marks his plaque.   40

39 JOHN ROSS (CHEROKEE) 1790–1866

Son of Daniel Ross from Sutherland, John Ross was to become the elected head of the first ever independent American Indian nation.

Although he and his people sided with General Jackson against the Creek Indians, Jackson would later turn on them.

The Cherokee nation had adopted European customs, built roads, schools and churches, and had a written constitution ratified by the US government. But when gold was found on their land, Jackson, now US President, had them cleared to appease his electorate.

The 'Trail of Tears' survives in the oral tradition. Survivors also sent money to help Scottish Highlanders emigrate.

Glossary/Explication

LINES 1–2 John Ross, with the Cherokee in the war of 1812, fought side by side with General Jackson against Creek Indians at Horseshoe Bend. When Jackson became President, he would betray them. See also Alexander MacGillivray (20).

LINES 3–6 Rossville – named after himself. 'Moral modes' – The Cherokee had assimilated many European-style customs. They built roads, schools and churches (many became baptists), and were farmers and cattle ranchers. Many of them spoke Gaelic.

LINE 7–16 In 1828 the Cherokee were the first American Indian nation to have a written language and a constitution, guaranteeing them perpetual rights to their land and recognising the right to self-government. This was modelled on the Constitutional Congress of the USA. See John Witherspoon (9). The American government, however, refused to number the Cherokee State's star on the national flag, not regarding them as 'True Americans'. When gold was discovered on their native land, Jackson promised Georgian whites that if they voted for him, he would have the Cherokee removed.

LINES 17–24 When the Indian Removal Bill was passed by Jackson in 1828, the Cherokees were not allowed to dig for gold even on their own land. John Ross made a petition of 16,000 signatures, which was illegally rejected. When John returned, his eviction had taken place. Davy Crockett (who also had Scottish connections) lost his seat in Congress for opposing Jackson's views on Indian removal.

LINES 25–36 Seven thousand US soldiers went to remove the Cherokee but 1,000 escaped to the Great Smoky Mountains. Four thousand died, including John's wife Quatie, on the winter march to Oklahoma. The US Army would not allow them to bury their dead on the trail. When the people saw them they cried. It therefore became known as the 'Trail of Tears'. I have compared this with the unjust removal of the MacGregors of Glenstrae in 1603 after Glen Fruin. The descendants of those Cherokees who escaped to the Great Smoky Mountains have now bought their land back in North Carolina and make money from 'Whites' in gambling saloons. The descendants of those who went to Oklahoma have discovered fountains of oil on their reservation and cannot be evicted by law.

LINES 37–40 In Oklahoma, the Cherokee sent money to Scotland at the time of the potato famine to assist their brother Gaels in coming over to join them.

JOHN ROSS (CHEROKEE)

This Cherokee and clansman's laddie,
Did check bold Creeks, with Jackson's army,
But took in peace time to translating,
And schools increased right through his nation,
Then built with Rossville, road and church,   5
Fulfilling moral mode and thrust.
His ratified republic standing
Dissatisified the public's planning.
When hardened Georgians groped for gold,
'Twas Jackson for them sold his soul.   10
Ten thousand rowdy rushers panning,
Came down sae loudly crushing, clanging.
The Cherokee did start no fight,
Since men decreed they had no rights.
Their star not on the star-clad banner,   15
Debarred all from their part as partners.
But John did turn with might and mission
To Washington, with signed petitions,
Of sixteen thousand native names,
Which picked he out from pain-filled plains,   20
While Davy Crockett lost his seat
For staying staunch with John the Chief.
Though on return, in grim eviction,
John Ross ne'er spurned his firm conviction.
So seven thousand frightful troopers,   25
Descended, ousting like cruel looters.
Like brave Clan Gregor of Glenstrae,
Their braves as beggars walked enslaved.
Refusing rigs, horse, coach or cart,
These fugitives of noble hearts,   30
Into the setting sighing sun,
Did croon their dead and dying ones.
Though scores ran home by Smoky Mountains,
Through Oklahoma more claimed fountains.
Though many met foul deaths on route,   35
Those settled, set down second roots.
To Scotland, they sent some saved pennies,
For costly care, to cover, ferry
And help their brother Gaels so dear,
Prevent mair mothers' trails o' tears.   40

40 ROBERT NAPIER 1791-1876

From Dumbarton, Robert Napier came from an established family of blacksmiths, engineers and millwrights. After an apprenticeship with his father and Robert Stevenson, he went into business for himself designing marine engines. He quickly gained a good reputation and successful contracts.

He partnered with a Canadian, Samuel Cunard, to start the first transatlantic steamer mail service. With no backing from England, he and some Glasgow businessmen risked all, which succeeded in gaining him Admiralty contracts. He designed and built the world's first ferry for steam trains.

Although honoured by Europe's hierarchy, Britain never honoured him.

He is regarded as the Father of Shipbuilding on the Clyde.

Glossary/Explication

LINES 1-4 From his own memoirs and in his own words.

LINES 5-8 He was an apprentice with his father before he moved to Edinburgh, where he worked with Robert Stevenson (29), or 'Lighthouse Robert'.

LINES 9-12 With the £50 that his father lent him, he rented premises at Greyfriars Wynd off the High Street in Glasgow, and took on two apprentices.

LINES 13-16 Henry Bell was an engineer who launched Europe's first commercial steamboat. Napier acknowledged Bell's pioneering work. He won the Clyde Steamboat Race, where the *Clarence* and the *Helensburgh* had Napier engines.

LINES 17-20 James and his brother George formally worked with Napier as a blacksmith but went on to form J & G Thomson, which became John Brown's shipyard on the Clyde. The paddle sloop, the *Bernace,* beat the Thames-built consort *Atlanta* by 18 days on their maiden passages to India.

LINES 21-24 Samuel Cunard, a Nova Scotia businessman and ship owner, planned a regular transatlantic liner service and decided to come to Scotland for ships. Napier soon convinced Cunard that only large and powerful ships would meet his needs. The contract eventually provided for four 420 HP, 1150 ton ships, one of which, the *Caledonia*, was built in Dumbarton.

LINES 25-26 The 'Naperian' vacuum coffee machine was first of its kind and had two removable glass bowls.

LINES 27-34 With little support from English investors, a group of Glasgow friends and businessmen floated the British and North American Royal Mail Steam Packet Coy, leading naval contracts for the paddle sloops *Vesuvius* and *Stromboli*. Napier's engines were cheaper and more reliable than those from the English yards. The embarrassed Admiralty thereafter had Napier as a regular contractor. The iron steamers were called *Jackal, Lizard* and *Bloodhound.*

LINES 35-36 The world's first ferry for steam trains, the *Leviathan*, sailed between Edinburgh and Fife.

LINES 37-40 Napoleon III appointed Napier a Royal Commissioner at the Paris Exhibition, and he was presented to Empress Eugenie. He was consulted and respected by governments all over Europe, receiving high honours from France and Denmark but never honoured by Britain. He is considered the Father of Clyde Shipbuilding.

ROBERT NAPIER

'Twas out in dark coasts Robert suffered,
Whilst counting lampposts for his supper,
And started high a life sae lengthy
Embarking by the Clyde sae earthy
He gladly gathered guidance often,   5
From father and from Lighthouse Robert,
Which mighty mentors made him great,
For Clyde would ken his fame and fate.
With fifty pounds his father lent him,
A firm he'd found to start inventing,   10
Where honest ways would play their part,
For novices who'd make their mark.
His mind of dreams he'd tether well,
To pioneering Henry Bell's
Great work, from which he built an engine   15
For his yacht, which did win a mention.
James Thomson pounded sparks as smith,
From whom John Brown's guid yard still sits,
Which helped in haling India's ace,
That led unladen in that race.   20
By Cunard, cruised a west-bound vessel,
Through blue and looming crests to wrestle
And face by phase great gaps gigantic,
By blazing brave trails transatlantic.
On board such ships hot steam's song softly,   25
Was poured out with cauld cream on coffee.
When England withdrew cash as backer,
He linked then with Cunard as partner,
But proved his pureness, building sloops,
That surely shewed nae guilt but good.   30
'More value than from English yards,'
The Admiralty did regard
And aye concede with rude reluctance,
Since iron steamers proved their function.
A steam train ferry – Forth for Fife,   35
Would meet wi' many folks both sides.
No less esteemed in states in Europe,
Empress Eugenie gave him new hope.
Yet Britain's barons ne'er him cried
Shipbuilding Father o' the Clyde.   40

41 SIR WILLIAM DRUMMOND STEWART
1795–1871

*Born in Perthshire, the son of a Highland laird, William Drummond
Stewart was the Errol Flynn of Scottish history, much more hon-
oured in America than in Scotland, where he is now forgotten.*

*Yet he led wild explorations in Turkey, the Russian Steppes,
Tashkent, the Aral Sea, Georgia, the Crimea and Spain.*

*In America he pioneered the Oregon trail and was an intelligence
operative. He also introduced Native Americans and buffaloes to
the Perthshire hills, sponsored scientific and artistic explorations
of the untamed American West and was manfully heroic in
Victorian mould.*

*This 'Laird of the Wild West' is immortalised on canvas by
Alfred Jacob Miller.*

Glossary/Explanation

LINES 1–4 'The mighty Quinn' refers to the great versatile actor Anthony Quinn, who
played roles in many nationalities, and was a contemporary of the swash-buckling,
more type-cast actor, Errol Flynn, whose antics off-screen were were just as wild as they
were on screen.

LINES 5–6 He spent his childhood climbing the Grampians and riding. As an officer in the
Hussars, he led a victorious charge against the French Lancers at the Battle of Waterloo.

LINE 7–8 In 1820, after Army service, Stewart travelled the continent, through Italy,
Turkey, across the Russian Steppes, Persia, Tashkent, Samarkand, the Aral Sea,
Armenia, Georgia and the Crimea, before touring battle sites in Spain.

LINES 9–10 At his family's London address at Eaton Place, he was the favourite of the
duchess's daughter at numerous parties, balls, and functions.

LINES 11–20 He married a Perthshire lass at home, then approached the Foreign Office
offering his services as an intelligence operative. He became involved in fur trading with
Indians and fur trappers. With only limited equipment listed, he travelled through the
Appalachians, Ohio, Indiana and Illinois, shooting for game and food. Spring gather-
ings that year with the mountain men and Indians is highlighted in the verses.

LINES 21–24 In May 1833, Stewart became a hunter and a food supplier to lengthy wagon
convoys and prairie ships. 'Panna-hat' – Panama hat, which he wore with tartan trews.

LINES 25–30 He kept good order throughout all dangers and excelled at the hunt. He
lived wildly amongst many tribes, getting drunk and womanising nightly. See also (Jarl)
Henry Sinclair (1), Alexander MacGillivray (20), Alexander Mackenzie (24), John Ross
(Cherokee) (39), and David Douglas (43).

LINES 31–32 Throughout all this, he was gathering intelligence. With autumn coming,
he rode alone to Hudson's Bay outpost in Canada, where he made a full intelligence
report, which was dispatched back to Whitehall.

LINES 33–34 He was one of the principal pioneers of the Oregon Trail.

LINES 35–38 Besides buffalo, he took home bears, birds, plants, seeds, numerous west-
ern artefacts, a half breed and two red Indian braves. Those two half-breed Indians got
up to all sorts of drunken pranks.

LINE 39–40 Grantully, pronounced 'Grantly', lies on Strathtay, east of Aberfeldy, in
Perthshire.

SIR WILLIAM DRUMMOND STEWART

You might have seen the mighty Quinn,
Or fighting scenes o' flighty Flynn,
But Perthshire's heartland held their equal,
Whose feral acts I'll tell in sequel.
Though rough he grew by ben and glen,   5
At Waterloo he led his men,
Then played wild games far east o' Baltic,
And Asia, Spain, in feasts o' frolics.
At London's house, in Eaton Place,
With love and power, he'd keep the pace,   10
Yet underwent he next denying,
His government had sent him spying,
To journey with a pony, plaidie,
A gun with dirk, and scope, ne'er safely,
Through Appalachia to Ohio,   15
And gad for game on rudest high roads.
Exchanging whisky, knives, traps, clothing,
When trading trinkets, hides, and boasting,
Night campfire tales, horse racing, brawling,
Light dancing, ale, squaws, caber tossing,   20
Whilst panning for his wagon crews,
In Pana-hat, in tartan trews,
And buckskin bared for fitting chest,
Tae usher prairie ships out west.
Through wilderness, wet mountain ranges,   25
High rivers, desert droughts and rages,
Concurring more with native roots,
Yon buffalo with bear he'd shoot.
Through camps of Sioux and Snake, or Bannock,
He partied through a haze of havoc.   30
Through merriment out west unfettered,
Intelligence, he'd send by letter,
Then often trod to make new trails,
Aye Oregon! his name should hail.
To climb the hill-land breed and roam,   35
Ten bison William steered back home,
With grass-seeds, bears, new trees and plants,
And half-breed braves who'd reel and rant.
His lass sae worthy yet stayed canny,
At Castle Murthly then at Grantully.   40

42 JAMES GORDON BENNETT 1795–1872

Born in Keith and raised in seminary Catholic education, James Gordon Bennett founded the world's first democratic, publicly funded newspaper.

Working as a teacher in Washington, then as a newspaper correspondent, he decided to start his own paper, called the New York Herald, *which was to shape many of the methods of modern journalism, introducing stocks, society page, telegraph news and illustrations.*

His eloquence, wit and brass gained him a boycott followed by a landslide readership clientele. This 'Napoleon of the Newspaper' declared, 'I tell the honest truth in my paper, and I leave the consequences to God.'

Glossary/Explication

LINES 1–4 *Flite* – to flout, cheer, wrangle, or reprimand (Scots). James brandished his pen, in his own words, 'like a Highland claymore', for it was a combative arena that he dominated.

LINES 5–8 He was from a seminary-educated Roman Catholic monastic background, a practice once banned by penal laws. But here he would have free speech. He extended his education to voracious reading, especially in the emerging Romantics. He emigrated to the United States in 1819, lean and hungry, and began to earn a living as a teacher and swift, forceful writer on assorted cultural, economic and political topics for newspapers in Charleston and New York City.

LINES 9–34 In 1835, after a stint as Washington correspondent for the *New York Courier and Enquirer*, Bennett founded the *New York Herald* on a capital of $500, initially serving not only as editor and owner, but as the entire staff. The *Herald* appeared daily (a relatively new practice at the time) and sold for one cent per copy, and daringly aimed at self-support through large circulation and advertising at a time when papers lived only through subsidies by political parties or businesses. Bennett broke new ground by filling the paper with news from police courts, sporting fields, theatres, first-rate coverage of national and international events, and he both reported and made use of the latest technological innovations. By 1860 great steam presses were daily stamping out 50,000 copies of each day's paper. And each edition was full of the latest news gathered by telegraph, mail trains, and ocean steamers. It was the world's first tabloid newspaper. It was also the first to publish stocks and shares news. Both the steam press and the telegraph were Scottish inventions. LINE 33 'Usual mail' – post coming by steam ferry and by train.

LINES 35–40 He was the dynamo of the whole enterprise, delivering abrasive opinions on everything, declaring himself the 'Napoleon of the Newspaper', as the man who had infused it with 'life growing eloquence, philosophy, taste, sentiment, wit and humour'. 'New Democracy' was a term used to depict Jackson's administration. Bennett did not create the social circumstances that generated a democratic readership, but his combination of genius and brass were ideally suited to Jacksonian era journalism.

JAMES GORDON BENNETT

Just what exceeds the sword sae mighty
When forming steely thoughts tae flite wi',
Which like a claymore wields sae wildly,
But strikes and stains the leaf sae lightly?
From banned beliefs, to selling news,   5
A man frae Keith would ken these clues,
Who in the New World, linked at will,
This thinking through, with ink and quill.
Great gall with grit, his gifted writing
Made politics with wit exciting.   10
As Washington's best correspondent,
That Scottish son ne'er was despondent,
So saved up dollars, fuelling fame,
In favour of that gruelling game.
In New York City at this juncture,   15
This news-hawk fitly carried culture.
His *Herald* hotly for this cause,
One cent per copy for the cost
Would proffer for his institution,
Good profit from their distribution.   20
Since adverts e'er enlarged his base,
Ne'er adverse were his catholic tastes.
With views from police courts, drama, sports,
Sad news of recourse, scandal, stocks,
Events abroad, and of his nation,   25
He'd tell for all, with explication.
Ne'er few got better readers' treats
When New York's *Herald* reached the streets.
Some fifty thousand copies daily,
Were swiftly, soundly sought sae sarely.   30
The telegraph and steam press seamed,
Did spell of ardent fearless dreams,
And methods made by usual mail –
Aye Bennett blazed a New World trail.
That bold and often real shrewd shaker,   35
Napoleon of the Newspaper,
Through sentiment to pick and choose,
Pure eloquence with quip did fuse,
Which true technocracy perfected,
And New Democracy reflected.   40

43 DAVID DOUGLAS 1798–1834

Born in Scone, David Douglas went from being local estate gar-
dener to becoming one of the greatest botanical explorers ever.

Commissioned by the London Horticultural Society, he went to
eastern Canada then to the wilder north-west, exploring the Rockies
and eventually sending home 800 species of plant.

His next journey was to the south through the Sacramento
Valley.

An attempt to reach Alaska was thwarted by the grief of his canoe
capsizing and losing seeds.

He died in Hawaii but left us with 200 plants of his own name,
including the famous Douglas Fir tree.

Glossary/Explication

LINES 1–6 The MacDuff Thanes of Fife held the hereditary right to place the crown
upon the ascending monarch's brow. 'That bluff black stane' – the controversial Stone
of Destiny, which the Gaels nowadays call *Clach Albain*, or the 'Stone of Scotland'.
There is a Gaelic rune transcribed on the stone which translates to 'The race of the free
Scots shall flourish, and if this prophecy be not false, where the Stone of Destiny is
found they shall prevail by the right of heaven.'

LINES 7–16 David had worked on the local estate as a gardener before moving to
Glasgow's Botanic Gardens, where he met professor William Hooker (a botanist) who
asked him to lead an expedition to look for plants in North America, starting with tame
eastern regions, looking for new kinds of fruit and vegetables.

LINES 17–26 This led to his more challenging adventure on the north-west seaboard,
round Cape Horn, where he embarked on a long voyage and began exploring the area
of Vancouver. He travelled 7,000 miles inland, mostly on foot, climbing the Rockies
(probably the first European to do so) and named a mountain 'Hooker', after his tutor,
and one was called after himself. *Stob* – prickle or peak, in this case mountain (Gaelic).
He sent back many hundreds of seeds, at least 200 of which were new discoveries and
130 were to flourish in Britain due to similar climates. He then travelled south by the
Columbia River, exploring the Sacramento Valley. This was followed by an abortive
attempt to reach Alaska. LINES 25–26 *Strath* – valley (Gaelic).

LINES 27–32 He lost all his seeds and instruments when his canoe capsized. 'Fair Alex'
– See Sir Alexander Mackenzie (24).

LINES 33–38 'Man o' Grass' – a name given to him by Natives. See also (Jarl) Henry
Sinclair (1), Alexander MacGillivray (20), John Ross (Cherokee) (39) and William
Drummond Stewart (41) for similar ethnic comparisons. He went to explore Hawaii,
but in 1833 he died unexpectedly when he fell in a pit trap dug for wild cattle, which
a bull had already fallen into and which gored him to death.

LINES 39–40 Two hundred plants bear his name. 'Firs o' fame' – the Douglas Fir.

DAVID DOUGLAS

In ancient times MacDuff alane
Did bear beside that bluff black stane
The crown upon the monarch's brow,
Tae tout the sovereign's lot that hour.
At Scone's old court, these noble deeds   5
With runes or odes, breathed olden creeds.
But seeds were planted in that place,
In recent and less distant dates.
A sower frae auld Scone e'er hallowed,
Would rove the feral woods then fallow,   10
Right where the New World's eastern seaboard
Arrayed with fruit-filled greenest leaf hoards.
He there collected plants in plenty,
Then went o'er west wi' plans o' entry
By stout great storms, through sea manoeuvres   15
Around Cape Horn, to reach Vancouver.
So fit and fleet, this fine explorer
Went inland seeking wildest flora,
Then came up through the northern Rockies,
To name anew some stobs sae stocky.   20
Eight hundred species sent he home,
Then up he'd rear again tae roam,
Whilst craving for more exploration,
Preparing for his next location.
Down through the Strath of Sacramento   25
He'd look sae hard for plant mementoes.
He almost made Alaska also,
But torrents bade that task sae hollow.
A full canoe this lion handled,
Back to Vancouver, plying paddles.   30
But on the Fraser River's rapids,
He lost his freight as did fair Alex.
This man o' grass and grief sae wiry,
Did land at last in green Hawaii,
But whilst exploring island tracts,   35
Alas was gored whilst tightly trapped
There by a wild and frightened bull
To die in vilest style sae cruel.
Yet dubbed he weel in his own name
Two hundred seeds with firs o' fame.   40

44 JAMES BOWMAN LINDSAY 1799–1862

*Born in Dundee, this school teacher is scarcely accredited for one of
the world's greatest inventions and yet clearly, in 1835, the news-
paper reports and many witnesses perceived what was obviously
the world's first perpetual electric light bulb being demonstrated
during lectures in one of Dundee's town halls.*

*But also looking at light in a spiritual context, he translated the
Lord's Prayer into 50 different languages in his Pentecontaglossal
Dictionary.*

*Astronomical table for the stars was manifested in his Chrono-
Astrolabe.*

*Anticipating wireless telegraphy he also initiated attempts to
conduct communications signals through salt water.*

Glossary/Explication

LINES 1–4 Illustrated by lighting a match in a dark room to note that the flame from
that match will supersede and the darkness will not engulf the light. This allegory is
equally true in a spiritual context.

LINES 5–8 Here I'm leading the narrative in the comparison with flame against some-
thing less odorous and smoky. 'Like the poet did say' – William McGonigall, who,
although known for his calypso-like disregard for metre, often mentioned the River Tay.

LINES 9–10 In 1835, Lindsay gave a series of public lectures at Thistle Hall in Dundee,
for what would be the first known perpetual light bulb.

LINES 11–20 The local newspapers wrote, 'Mr Lindsay succeeded on the evening of
Saturday 25 July in obtaining a constant electric light... The light in beauty surpasses
others, has no smell, emits no smoke, is capable of explosion and, not requiring air for
combustion, can be kept in sealed glass jars.' Lindsay replied: 'I am writing this letter
by means of it at six inches or eight inches distant, and... I can read a book at a dis-
tance of one and a half feet... I can make it burn in the open air or in a glass tube with-
out air and neither wind nor water is capable of extinguishing it.' LINE 14 Thomas
Edison eventually took the credit, or patent, for it.

LINES 21–24 Amongst many witnesses this display was for what would be the first per-
petual electric light bulb, which was hooded, or moulded, from an old jam jar.

LINES 25–30 Lindsay's Pentecontaglossal Dictionary would make the Lord's Prayer
readable in 50 different languages.

LINES 31–32 The Chrono-Astrolabe was a set of astronomical tables designed to aid in
the reckoning of time periods.

LINES 33–36 He attempted wireless transmission of messages across the Tay, using sea
water as a conductor for the signal. He was the first to propose it for international com-
munication. But telegraphic apparatus was to be further developed by another three
Scotsmen: Fredrick G. Creed, Alexander Graham Bell and Alexander Bain.

LINES 39–40 Part of my nova-riddle for the light bulb.

JAMES BOWMAN LINDSAY

We ken that light dispels all darkness,
Expelling strife and spells of sadness.
This ancient vision ne'er sae wordy,
Remains in wisdom e'er sae worthy.
But with bare fiery flames you'll find,   5
Their spit, their sigh, and shameless shine,
Just like the lightning o'er the Tay,
Skies brighten, like the poet did say.
But in a place called Thistle Hall,
Who lit that strange bald crystal ball?   10
'No smell, nor smoke, for folks to suffer,
Nor bellowed coke to choke or smother
But beauty that surpasses others.'
(Which surely that good man discovered.)
'This flame ne'er moves in flicker motion,   15
Since air ne'er brews nor brings explosions,
And cannot pierce this glassy vacuum,
All jammed or sealed in darkest darkroom.
For books to view from this light beaming,
A foot or two permits sight reading.'   20
Effective words the press would write,
Reflecting his electric light.
Much folk did gaze on this great glow,
Provoking praise for Lindsay's show.
But light which links with verse and spirit   25
With might, did give the earth a visit.
This gifted one with grace in patience,
In fifty tongues embraced the nations
In saving of the souls – revival
In prayer from the Holy Bible.   30
In gaps to gauge through star to star
His astrolabe could chart afar.
But waves through waves from shore to shore,
Would strain to say what's stored in store.
Communication claimed by cable   35
Would prove its patent status stable,
But his bright bulb and light so shiny,
Well lit right up that night so grimy.
That onion that will bring no tears,
Wi' sunny hat to fringe its ears.   40

45 JAMES CLARK ROSS 1800–1862

Nephew of Sir John Ross, James Clark Ross joined the Royal Navy aged 11 and joined his uncle on the voyage to charter the Magnetic North. He later embarked on a voyage to charter the Magnetic South Pole.

This most humane commander believed that his greatest asset was his men and had his two-ship expedition to the Magnetic South Pole especially fitted out with abundant rations of the best of food for his crew.

Through many hazards of storms and false starts he eventually claimed Antarctica for Queen Victoria. He named an ice shelf after her but later re-named it after himself.

Glossary/Explication

LINES 1–6 Joining the Royal Navy at the age of 11, he was tutored and watched over by his uncle, Sir John Ross (39). Together they charted the Magnetic North Pole.

LINES 7–14 On 8 April 1839, Ross took command of the 370 ton ship *Erebus*, with his friend Francis Crozier assuming command of the 340 ton *Terror*. Both ships were strengthened, and substantial supplies of preserved meat were loaded aboard to head off the risk of scurvy. In addition, extraordinary amounts of soups, vegetables, cranberries, pickles and other foodstuffs were included. Ross knew that a well-fed, comfortable crew was a happy crew, so extensive work was also done to the ships' interiors.

LINES 15–20 Ross sailed to Tasmania where he was to set up permanent stations for making magnetic observations at St Helena Island, the Cape of Good Hope and Tasmania. On route to Hobart, they met with Sir John Franklin and 200 convicts. See also Alexander Maconochie (36).

LINES 21–28 The hurricane separated the two ships and caused one fatality. LINE 27 That sea is now called the Ross Sea.

LINES 31–32 He named two of those mountains 'Erebus' and 'Terror', after the ships.

LINES 31–34 Iceberg mountains. Adapted quote from R. McCormick, ship's surgeon, and Dr Hooker's notes (see also David Douglas (43) notes on LINES 7–16), where we wrote, 'All the coast is one mass of dazzling beautiful peaks of snow, which when the sun approaches the horizon, reflected the most brilliant tints of golden yellow and scarlet, and then to see the dark cloud of smoke tinged with a flame, rising from the volcano... This was a sight so surpassing everything that can be imagined... that it really caused a feeling of awe to steal over us... our one comparative insignificance and helplessness, and at the same time, an indescribable feeling of the greatness of the Creator in the works of His hand.' The peak was over 12,000 feet high.

LINES 35–40 The Victoria Barrier, later renamed as the Ross Ice Shelf. The impassable barrier stretched as far as the eye could see. He claimed Antarctica for Queen Victoria in 1841.

JAMES CLARK ROSS

Whilst serving on his choicest charter,
Magnetic North, Sir John's well captured
Together with his friend and nephew,
Who'd help on trips to tend to rescues.
Give eyes or ears for those of yon age,   5
Who pioneered yon polar voyage!
To take his turn preparing plans,
Young James did come to bear command.
Two ships equipped with rations, rigging,
Would lift his witty tars with jigging,   10
For groups of food for all these worthies,
Like soups and fruit to halt the scurvy,
Would warm their hearts to help them hold
Through storm, in darkness, wet and cold.
Their goal would be the old Antarctic's   15
South Pole, through freezing foam Atlantic.
On Good Hope's Cape, and down in Hobart,
To prove those bearings sound and sober,
Their main magnetic observations,
They'd take and test in all their stations.   20
Whilst upping pace to Auckland's Isles,
A hurricane would rock and rile
Their ships right through a wild old gamble,
To bring them to the Isles o' Campbell.
Through vilest vexing wasteful gales,   25
By icebergs next they'd face blue whales.
While setting out to open sea,
Magnetic South's true course they'd keep.
At last Antarctic calmly loomed,
Like vast fantastic parrots plumes.   30
'Twelve thousand feet, crisp snowy bens,
Great towering peaks in golden red,
Clear glare of magma through grey smoke,
Creator's hand hath surely spoke.'
Their queen's white heights were next revealed,   35
Appearing like a pearly shield.
A season lost, he crossed the circle,
But freezing brought his cause to dwindle.
He'd hold his claim, this ode convinces,
As most humane o' polar princes.   40

Alexander Shanks was born in Arbroath, and grew up to be an engineer.

His local landlord commissioned him to design a lawnmower for his green.

He invented the Shank's Machine, which, when pulled by pony, rolled the grass as well as mowing it, therefore rolling over any foot or hoof marks.

Although he died young, his son took his invention to the Great Exhibition in London, which won him many famous high profile contracts such as Wimbledon tennis grounds, Lords cricket grounds and St Andrews Old Course.

His invention is the direct predecessor of the modern lawnmower.

Glossary/Explication

LINES 1–4 Here we have the imminent warning of the coming of late spring and early summer and what lies in store for those who have lawns or greens to maintain.

LINES 5–8 Description of grass shooting through the soil in early summer, compared with rapier foils (sword blades).

LINES 9–16 Invitation to be at the ready with your lawnmower and description of the procedure of mowing.

LINES 17–22 In 1841 Alexander was commissioned by his local laird to design a mower for his green, or lawn.

LINES 23–24 While credit is usually given to the Englishman Edwin Budding, Shanks is the inventor of the lawnmower, and his Shank's Machine was the direct predecessor of the modern lawnmower.

LINES 25–32 Earlier lawnmowers were pushed instead of pulled, and in doing so often churned up the ground. Shanks's Machine was pulled by a small pony without leaving any hoof marks, for it not only mowed, but also rolled the grass after it.

LINES 33–38 Although Shanks himself died at a young age, his son showed the mowers at the 1851 Great Exhibition in London, winning an award, and leading to the successful business that continued into the 20th century, supplying mowers to cut the grass of the tennis courts of Wimbledon, the cricket ground at Lords and the Old Course at St Andrews.

LINES 39–40 Adapted nova-riddle for the lawnmower.

ALEXANDER SHANKS

Though early summer's clear and calm,
Still yet we suffer sheer alarm.
Though sweet soft air our nostrils gauge,
Last season's rain's now wrought its rage.
When wet blades warp, then wake in soil,   5
Then stretch, then yawn, like rapier foils,
Their cheerful charms your shoes are meeting,
Whose green cool arms give you a greeting.
Controlling length and height be ready
To roll with strength, and sight sae steady,   10
And shove that plough that does nae splitting
Above flat ground, its turf resisting,
Its wheels or cogs on both sides strewing,
Do peel or crop all growth while chewing
The grass sae green upon the lawn,   15
Tae chant the season's chopping song.
An engineer in old Arbroath
Once lent his ears and swore an oath
To help his local laird to care wi'
Yon lengthy growth, and flail his fairway.   20
As handy man, this harrow-yoke,
Would Alexander Shanks promote,
Which yardstick surely should on platen,
Have had his blueprint proof of pattern.
As first indeed frae bush to bush,   25
His rig did need nae pull nor push
Nor truss tae trust, tae stiffly suffer,
Tae turn the turf, as did the others.
This plough-like yoke was pulled by pony,
Without a sole or shoe-print scoring,   30
For hoof marks would be rolled all over,
When oor man moved his bold lawnmower.
When Sandy sadly died, his son,
Ne'er handled badly, aye but won
Great Exhibition's sought award,   35
Famed tennis lists, auld lots at Lords,
St Andrews greens, which surely shewed,
That Shanks' Machine just could nae lose,
While birling blades aye blunted, blazing,
When bursting base tae bludgeon, baring.   40

47 JOHN PULLAR 1803–1878

John Pullar from Perth was a professional dyer and cloth fuller, and was the first ever person to introduce automated dry cleaning. He advertised as follows:

'Crepes, silks, velvets, poplins and bombazeens dyed and dressed on the most approved principles. British and foreign shawls and scarfs cleaned without injuring the most delicate colours. Chip straw and leghorn hats dyed and dressed, cloths dried and furniture of all kinds cleaned and renewed. Crumb cloths and all sorts of carpeting and hearth rugs cleaned and renovated to look like new.'

He produced a happy nationwide enterprise, remembered only now in name.

Glossary/Explication

LINES 3–8 A rhyming adaptation of their original advert. See his biography above.

LINES 9–14 John Pullar's neighbours in Burt Close complained of the 'nuisance' of his dyeing, forcing him to move. He settled on a piece of ground near the remains of Black Friars Monastery, where the enchanting Lade Burn was a good supply of water with essential purification qualities, which would enhance both dyeing and waste emissions.

LINES 15–20 Twenty years later, John's experienced son Robert joined his father in partnership, securing small agents in the area outwith Perth and even further afield.

LINES 21–24 'A Royal Warrant' – Dyer to Her Majesty the Queen, an accolade which would increase (now Robert's) business, resulting in the purchase of a range of machines and an increased workforce of 100, for later extension in Kinnoul Street for finishing and dry cleaning.

LINES 25–34 Robert's attitude towards his workforce was enlightened but paternalistic. He diffused the strike of 1873 by offering a 51-hour working week, dinner from 1–2pm, wages on Saturday at 1pm, changes in overtime and a general rise in wages. John Pullar died in 1878. Four years later, Robert bought the old Tulloch bleach works, cleared the site and built a modern factory. With cheaper postal rates, he opened up the English market, gaining offices in Brighton, Bath, Liverpool, Manchester, Newcastle and London, where there were three offices. The North British Dye Works at Tulloch employed a happy workforce, with recreational clubs and paid holidays. By 1890 his business empire extended the full length of Britain, with 4,000 agencies or outlets and the best conditions in the country for nearly 3,000 workers.

LINES 35–38 With union disputes, the rail strike, continued industrial action and the rise in food prices, the next 20 to 30 years caused Rufus Pullar to die at only 56, through the strain. This brought about the demise of the family business and a feeling of sadness amongst the workers.

LINES 39–40 'Lye' – used in early laundering. 'Fuller's earth' – a type of clay, anciently used to absorb soils and grease from cloth. The name 'Pullar' became synonymous with dry cleaning. Although the company was bought over by another firm, the brand name yet survives.

JOHN PULLAR

Don't fly away by steam express!
There's dry engagements here to press:
'Of crapes, fine foreign shawls, scarves, velvets,
Dark drapes, crumb cloth, leghorn hats, pelmets,
Bright bombazeens, hearth rugs, kemp carpets,   5
Fine straw-chip screens that come from markets,
Plain poplins, soft weave, household chattels,
Whose splotch wi' blotch we'll oust or tackle.'
When folks did blurt or sigh assurance,
The crones in Burt's Close cried out 'Nuisance!'   10
So o'er to Black Friars John did flit.
Where lore ne'er lacked wise thought nor wit,
For dyes did reap a distal daze,
Down by the clear and crystal Lade.
When twenty years were o'er and done,   15
He sent his eager only son
Into the business, bringing aid,
With pools of wisdom in the trade,
Who'd push on outset, round the county,
To boost new outlets, bound for bounty.   20
His call as dyer for the sovereign,
Would warrant higher profit oft, then
An east-side street near auld Kinnoul,
Saw dream machines clean cloth in full.
Though sadly John himself expired,   25
His lad resolved to ne'er retire.
When Tulloch's lot he bought and cleared,
Another poignant plot appeared.
Which ploy then did rebound to equal
Employment for three thousand people,   30
Best safety standards, and best wages,
For agent staff in farthest places.
Their fifty-one hour working week
Assisted somehow for their keep.
When civic work disputes did come,   35
Their business world endured a slump.
The chairman's death brought under strain,
Their day has left with but a name.
Though born in lye with fuller's earth,
Guid Scots yet cry it: Pullar's Perth.   40

Michael Nairn, born in Kirkcaldy, was descended from an unbroken line of master weavers whose thriving trade had picked up after the Napoleonic Wars. He was first apprenticed to James Cox, who became one of the jute barons of Dundee.

In 1847 he started his own floor-cloth company. With a massive bank loan, he built his first factory in Kirkcaldy but the struggle of getting the business established took its toll on his health and he died aged 54.

However, his wife continued the company, producing what was to be the first printed, patterned, coloured linoleum.

Glossary/Explication

LINES 1–6 *Thirled* – tethered (Scots). Michael's great-grandfather, Andrew Nairn, was Deacon of the Guild of Weavers and his grandfather worked in the weaving trade.

LINES 7–8 Destined for the weaving trade, Michael was apprenticed alongside James Cox, who later became one of Dundee's Jute Barons. In 1828 Michael opened a canvas weaving business in Coal Wynd, Kirkcaldy, making canvas for floor cloth.

LINES 9–14 In 1847 he borrowed £4,000 from bankers for construction of his first factory. He understood there would be no quick outlay as it took months for floor cloth to mature before it could be sold.

LINES 15–18 His first floor cloth factory was in Nether Street, on top of cliffs at Pathhead Sands, dubbed 'Nairn's Folly' by sceptics. There the cloth was dried by the heat of the sun from the south facing windows.

LINES 19–26 It was 1849 before he made any profit at all. The banks had great faith in him, for they loaned all the money throughout that period when he had no other partners or backers. Michael worked day and night running the business, travelling all over selling floor cloth. His efforts took their toll on his health and despite warnings to slow down, he died in 1858, aged 54.

LINES 27–30 The company continued to expand, with technical improvements and increased demands. His widow Catherine Ingram, his son Robert, and manager James Shepherd formed a partnership. In 1861 they were joined by another son, Michael Barker Nairn, and extensions were made to the 'Folly'. This encouraged other firms to be formed. At the 1862 Exhibition in London, and the 1867 Exhibition in Paris, Nairn's floor cloth came into its own and won many prizes.

LINES 31–36 In 1868 an added impetus for Nairn's was given by the establishment of Kirkcaldy's water supply, which provided a better source of power for the factories. The harbour was also vitally important for import of raw materials and export of finished goods.

LINE 37–40 From an old folk song about the linoleum works in Kirkcaldy. Burning linseed oil was used for the finishing process and could be smelled on the approaching train.

MICHAEL NAIRN

A keen, conformed or thirled believer,
And Deacon of the Guild of Weavers,
Did pass his passion, wisdom, skill,
And craft sae balanced with guid will,
Down to his grandson's brightest bairn   5
Whose good kin baptised Michael Nairn,
Whose stock-in-trade, talk, with some keys,
He got from James Cox in Dundee.
But when all training strains were over,
He then would raise his place as owner.   10
For brand new plans which he had sown,
This man would start to seek a loan
For costs outweighing all he bade
In long outlay, with loss repaid.
Near Pathhead Sands, by fair Kirkcaldy,   15
His park was branded 'Nairn's Folly',
Where patterned cloth did hang in sunlight
To matt in mothless stands sae upright.
Much faith in him did place yon bankers,
Who'd rate him with the rare top rankers.   20
Undaunted, here and there he'd run,
Till dawn did greet setting sun.
When labours took their toll unfairly,
Health dangers shook his soul up sarely.
Though by the doctors warned then cautioned,   25
He died with long-term drawn exhaustion.
His firm in name, still mair expanding,
Confirmed its fame with craved demanding.
Their key extensions marking pace,
Did keep abreast with market's race.   30
With all day water power coming,
The 'Folly' got more hours of running,
And basic source goods used, in vogue,
Did Nairn's import into the port,
To export patterned printed rolls,   35
That yet does flatter finished floors.
'He chakkit tickets, gein them back',
Folk a' did sing on steely tracks,
And 'Next stop's in Kirkcaldy', sung,
When scent of sickly oil did burn.   40

Born in Forres, Hugh Falconer became Superintendent of Saharánpur Botanic Gardens in India. With the help of three Scotsmen – Robert Fortune, Dr William Jameson and the marketing skill of Thomas Lipton – he successfully transplanting tea from China to India, to become the drink of the British Empire.

Until then, China had been the main supplier of tea, but Robert Fortune disguised himself as a Chinese boy and infiltrated China, transporting tens of thousands of plants over the Himalayas into India, where they were grown and improved by Jameson, marketed by Thomas Lipton, and brought to breakfast tables worldwide.

Glossary/Explication

LINES 1–2 Tea has now become part and parcel of our breakfast.

LINE 3–4 'Billy-can' is a cylindrical tin or enamel container used as a kettle, cooking pot or food carrier, especially in Australia and New Zealand of the old British Empire, from whence the term came.

LINES 9–12 We now associate most tea with India, but before Hugh Falconer was appointed Superintendent of the Saharánpur Botanic Gardens in 1832, tea was imported from China.

LINES 13–20 The rush was on to find a more economical route and defuse the Chinese monopoly. LINES 15–16 *Sleekit* – sly (Scots). 'Chime wi' China', i.e. be as good as, if not better than, Chinese tea. The north-western Himalayan foothills appeared to be climatically suited for tea plantations.

LINES 21–28 Robert Fortune was a plant collector who was commissioned to infiltrate China. To do so he disguised himself either as a cleric or a peasant boy with a shaved head, but kept a ponytail and gave himself a Chinese name. On the first trip he survived pirates in the Yellow Sea, gale force winds and lynch mobs. The second trip was more overt and profitable but less dramatic. He was commissioned by the East India Company, who were also Falconer's employers.

LINES 29–34 Fortune oversaw the transporting of tens of thousands of plants and seedlings over the Himalayas, to places including Hakkim, Assam and Darjeeling. He also brought Chinese tea growers with him.

LINES 35–36 Falconer's successor in the Botanic Gardens, Dr William Jameson, improved the crop and beefed up production to the point where Indian tea replaced Chinese on the breakfast tables of Britain.

LINES 37–38 Thomas Lipton, who marketed from his Glasgow grocer's shop, became the international brand name associated with tea. He opened his first shop in Glasgow in 1871. His artistic posters, still regarded as curiosities, led him into opening more branches in Glasgow, then expanded his business into England and the USA. With competitive pricing, innovative and arty packaging in tins to keep the tea fresh, quirky advertising; and being able to blend teas according to tastes, he dominated the world market.

LINE 40 Adaptation of my nova-riddle for tea.

HUGH FALCONER

So steadfast is old leafy tea
With breakfast, in those B&Bs,
Or billy-cans for entire camps
On hilly lands of empire's stamp.
Like many tastes from parts or places,   5
This scented savoured char e'er chases
That burning thirst from throat or lip,
While slurping with a sole hot sip.
From India, it was believed,
Originated yon green leaf.   10
But did it here though roil its roots
When lifting seed through soil in shoots?
In Saharanpur's greenest gardens,
A gardener's avid dreams imagined:
'Let's seek a sleekit line that's finer,   15
For cheaper tea tae chime wi' China's,
By tracking back with some tea plants,
And farm them fast in lush, free land,
By foothills of the Himalayas,
Which fruitful thought will trip or pay us.'   20
A man named Fortune from auld Berwick,
Was garbed in costume of a cleric
Or peasant boy, whose head was cropped,
And sent deployed, to check for stocks.
His second trek was more overt,   25
And set to settle or convert
Economy or greater trading,
That caused yon claim to fame ne'er fading.
On Sherpas backs, tea plants and seedlings
Did trek by track to grand Darjeeling,   30
To Hakkim and Assam's plantations,
To start this class art adaptation,
That e'er resounds as epoch label,
That's yet renowned on people's tables.
For Hugh's successors on the scene,   35
Would move with measures for his dream.
Aye Lipton, Glasgow flew the flag
For sifted char, stored loose in bags,
Transformed to truly tempt and try
Those toffs who toured in tents tongue-tied.   40

50 JAMES NASMYTH 1808–1890

*Born in Edinburgh, James Nasmyth's school friend's father owned
an iron foundry, which he would visit. At the age of 15 he began
exploring the steam engine whilst making models and selling them.*

*After a short meeting with London toolmaker Henry Maudslay, he
opened a foundry in Manchester, inventing many safety-orientated
tools. But his greatest invention was the steam hammer, which,
although extremely powerful, could crack an eggshell in a wine
glass with precision; forge iron plates for warships; or simply
hammer in a nail.*

*This cost-effective invention helped build bridges, quays and
was very labour-saving.*

Glossary/Explication

LINES 1–6 Whilst at school, James was friendly with a boy whose father owned an iron
foundry, which James visited weekly. He began developing the steam engine at the age
of 15 by building his own models for sale.

LINES 7–10 In 1829 he took a working model plus drawings of a small steam engine
to London to show Henry Maudslay, a toolmaker and engineer, who was so impressed
by his skill that he took him on as an apprentice. 'Moon maker' – when James eventu-
ally retired he built 'Moon Art', models of the moon. A large illustrated volume with
plates of the simulated moon's surface was produced with James Carpenter in 1874.

LINES 11–14 Maudslay died suddenly in 1831 and by the end of the year James returned
to Edinburgh to produce his own engineering tools, then moved to Manchester, renting
part of an old cotton mill until the increasing weight of the machinery caused its floor
to collapse.

LINES 15–26 In 1836 he opened the Bridgewater Foundry, beside the canal and the
Liverpool-Manchester railway. He invented the foundry ladle, useable by just one man
rather than 12, thus minimising the risk of accidents from the spillage of molten metal.
He also invented everything else listed in the verses.

LINES 27–38 It was here that he built the famous steam hammer, described as 'one of
the most perfect artificial machines and noblest triumphs of mind over matter'. He had
received a request from Brunell, the railway and shipbuilding tycoon, to forge a drive
shaft to power the huge paddle wheels for his proposed ship ss *Great Britain*. So
Nasmyth invented the steam hammer, which could be controlled and adjusted with
such precision as to break an eggshell inside a wine glass and leave the glass intact. The
steam hammer was employed wherever there was heavy industry because of its ability
to apply controlled powerful force. It could be used, for example, to hammer a nail or
forge iron plates for warships.

LINES 39–40 Nasmyth applied the same principle to the production of a pile driver
used in constructing bridges, quays and harbours, and for piling the foundations of all
kinds of masonry. It was used in the building of the high level bridge in Newcastle and
the naval dockyards at Devonport.

JAMES NASMYTH

Aye making toy trains for his tracks
Prepared this boy's brain for the knack
Of fitting rivets into seams,
Fast hitting, driven with pure steam.
Those trains which tracked in hard hot engines,   5
Regaled the arts and crafts conventions.
But one of those, he brought his way
To London's Maudslay for display,
Who though himself a guid toolmaker,
Made known his bent to this moon maker.   10
But sadly death befell old Henry,
So Nasmyth went on next to help wi'
The fittings of all sorts to fill out
The building of a cotton mill-house.
A works there too he called Bridgewater,   15
Would turn fair tools, in yon dim corner,
Where James did make his sound with stable
And caring, safety foundry ladle,
Produced with skill to pour sae settled,
Reducing spills of molten metal.   20
To test his will and craft he'd plan:
A flexible drive shaft, steam ram,
An engine cutting, shaping keys,
Hard self-adjusting bearings, wheels,
Hydraulic press, hand drills, nut-milling,   25
In awesome tests, that skill fulfilling.
His vision, like a towering light,
Precision, pride with power and might,
Will, wisdom, skill with native wit
All linked, would bring a greater gift.   30
For so exact was this great jack,
'Twould blow, bend, bash, warp, twist, break, hack,
Yet crack an eggshell in a glass,
Ne'er jabbing ends, with stem bypassed.
This blatant seething stark dream rammer,   35
He'd patent freely as steam hammer,
Which nailed and forged big iron plates
On naval warships tied to state.
More great hard tools of many kinds,
This Brainheart duly well designed.   40

APPENDIX I — THE METRICAL MIRROR

An expanded explanation of its background, system and ethos.

Technically, the definition of the *Metrical Mirror* might be summed up thus:

A fusion of ancient battle metres and rhymes from medieval Gaelic clan poetry (though used here in Scots/English) whereby the vowel on each second pulse of the heartbeat corresponds in rhyme (and in a few cases half-rhyme), and metre with the vowel immediately above or below (vertically) in the couplet, both internally and terminally, often embellished with added assonance and alliteration.

Here is an example of internal vowels corresponding in sound with the ones within the line immediately above or below, and terminal vowels corresponding in sound with the ones at the end of each line above or below.

This is from 'Lament to Clanranald' (*Marbhrann do Mhac 'ic Ailein*) who died of his wounds at the Battle of Sherrifmuir in 1715. The poet remembers his bravery in the time of battle as the revered leader of his men.

Here, I have highlighted the vowel stresses:

Marcaich sunndach nam pillean
Air each cruidheach nach tilleadh
Nach d' gabh curram no giorradh
Nuair a dhublaich an tine

Lively rider of the saddle-cloths
On the shod horse that would not turn back
who would not be anxious nor alarmed
when the firing was doubled

Here is an example from the same bard (John MacDonald of Benbecula), called 'The Song of the Highland Clans' (*Oran nam Fineachan Gaidhealach*), from 1715:

'S i seo'n aimsir an dearbhar and targanach dhuinn
's bras meanmach fir Alba fon armaibh air tus
nuair a dh'eireas gach treunfhear' na eideadh glan ur
le run feirg' agus gairge gu seirbheis a'chruin

This is the time when the prophecy will be fulfilled for us.
With our men of Scotland mettlesome and spirited, armed in the van of the battle
When each valiant man will rise in brand new garb
With angry fierce determination in the service of the crown

This style, in quadrant verse, is being used as an incitement to battle, for the Jacobite Rising of 1715. (See also notes on James Francis Edward Keith (5)). Here it's clear to see that the rhyming vowel stresses mark out the pace of the metre. Those eulogies and elegies were designed for the praise of human virtues and incitements which were salutary, captivating glimpses of marshal imagery. But have those ingredients been used in epic tale-telling until now?

On the other hand, the rhyming couplets used by Blind Harry's 'The Wallace', Robert Burns's 'Tam O'Shanter' and Barbour's 'The Bruce' are component parts of the greater narrative.

Here is an example from Burns's tale, 'Tam O'Shanter':

But to our tale: Ae market night,
Tam had got planted unco right,
Fast by an ingle, bleezing finely,
Wi' reaming swats that drank divinely...

Here the major rhyme as such is mostly terminal, that is, the last major vowel at the end of each line on the couplet, as also in this example from Blind Harry's 'The Wallace':

But Wallace he march'd stoutly through the plain,
Led on his men, their number did disdain;
Till Warren's host thick on the edge did go,
Then he from Jop did take the horn and blow:

'The Wallace' is composed in *iambic pentameter*, that is, five minor and major heartbeats to each line, therefore 10 in each couplet. 'Tam O'Shanter', on the other hand, is constructed in *iambic tetrameter*, that is, four minor and major heartbeats in each line, and eight in each couplet.

To illustrate this metre, I've taken the same piece as above, from 'Tam O'Shanter', highlighting the major (every second) heartbeat.

But to our tale: Ae market night,
Tam had got planted unco right,
Fast by an ingle, bleezing finely,
Wi' reaming swats that drank divinely...

There are two noteworthy differences from that of Gaelic hero verse. In the Gaelic, the stressed vowels overtly correspond or rhyme, but here in 'Tam O'Shanter', not so much so, with the exception of the terminal major vowel of each couplet. Notably, quite often the consonants of the terminal word of each couplet also correspond. This is quite often not the case in Gaelic hero verse, since the Gaelic language, by its very nature, contains vowels which are more stressed and often overshadow the consonant soundings.

So, if we blend all of these ingredients of metre, internal rhyme, terminal rhyme, make the major vowels correspond with each other in each corresponding couplet, spice it up with further consonant rhyme *(alliteration)* as well as further vowel rhyme *(assonance)*, have each couplet so that it might be a self-contained statement but be a component part of the whole story, then we have what I have christened the *Metrical Mirror.*

The Metrical Mirror

Here is an example of the *Metrical Mirror* from *The Prologue:*

What **ai**ls us **a**ll at t**u**nnel's end.
The day must d**aw**n for **u**s to mend.

Here, I have highlighted the corresponding vowels to show the unison of the pacing, but below in the same couplet, I have marked out the second or major heartbeats *(iambic)* of the four footed beat of each line *(tetrameter)* in syllables by capitalising them:

What-AILS-us-ALL-at-TUN-nel's-END,
The-DAY-must-DAWN-for-US-to-MEND.

This couplet has what is known in metrical terms as a *masculine* ending.

Below is an example of a couplet from the *Prologue* with a *feminine* ending:

Al-THOUGH-from-NOB-le-BONDS-be-GOT-*ten*,
At-HOME-your-SOUL-is-LONG-for-GOT-*ten*

The different between a masculine ending and a feminine ending is that the feminine ending has an added terminal half-syllable, in this case the syllable '*ten*'.

We could not have such an epic piece such as this without alliteration.

Here is an example of alliteration also from 'The Prologue':

Your **f**ame has **f**lown to **f**ar **f**lung corners
But maimed at home through tiresome scorners

This is a very overt example of a couplet with a feminine ending and alliteration. This one has corresponding 'f's in the top line (horizontally), although not in the second line (vertically) but nevertheless still keeping the corresponding internal mirror (vowel) rhyme (vertically).

Here's a more extreme couplet, from Alexander Shanks (46), which has the corresponding consonant on both:

While birling blades aye blunted, blazing,
When bursting base tae bludgeon, baring.

However, the vast majority of couplets are quieter.

So although I have utilised ancient rhyming techniques from Gaelic propagandist poetry, yet have composed in Scots/ English, for the most part, the mood of the couplets is one of a lighter nature, perkier, often quirky, and in some cases even caricatured. With added old sayings, new ones, ancient and modern riddles, quotations from poets, the Bible, philosophy, historical events, genealogies, traditional allegiances, folklore, customs, occupations and ethics, told in classical as well as modern diction, we have undertones mirroring or echoing a modern story still unsevered from ancient roots, embracing the ingenious, the courageous, and the bizarre.

In the hero ages, warriors would strike on their shields with the hilts of their swords in time to the rhythm of these chants that the bards would declaim before engaging in battle. Throughout peacetime pursuits, people at work in the fields, or those waulking (milling) cloth by hand, or those rowing boats, might have chanted out various types of heroic verses to help them pass the time, in what otherwise might have proved to be tedious or irksome chores. All of this served the purpose of exercising their memory recall, and to remind them of those with whom they were historically identified. They were inspired by a feeling of ancestral kinship, hence being identified with their heroic virtues and regenerating a heightened sense of self-dignity.

So there we have the *Metrical Mirror*, which, like a rhetoric reflection, echoes in pairing rhyme like an incantation or a battle stanza, signifying and echoing from the modern, hailing back to the heroic and most ancient times.

It is like a warp and weft of word weaving (coloured yarns woven at right angles to each other), keeping to the same sett (or pattern or motif), which might be likened unto tartan cloth production.

The sounding of each couplet might be envisaged as looking into a loch on a clear still day, with mountains and trees above it on the ground but equally reflected in the clear still cool water of the mid-morning daylight. This system also fits philosophically and phonetically with the essence of this epic exercise, in that this is a rhetoric reflection of the age of innovation or a double echo from the more remote past. This system marches like time itself, balancing the beat of battle with brain and heart.

THE ACROSTIC

The piece written for Robert Burns (19) has an added feature. As well as being in *metrical mirror,* it is also in the form of a rhyming acrostic, which simply reads:

RABBIE–BURNS-A-MANS-A-MAN-FOR-A-THAT-AULD-LANG-SYNE
This is exactly 40 letters.

Finally, in Robert Burns's 'Tam O' Shanter', there are exactly 200 lines, which means 100 couplets. Interestingly, 50 of those couplets have masculine endings and 50 feminine. In this book there are 50 innovators with 40 lines each = 2,000 lines + 40 lines for the prologue page = 2,040 lines = 1,020 couples. Exactly half of those have masculine endings and half have feminine endings. Therefore this piece is 10 times the length of 'Tam O'Shanter', and each piece would average 10/10 masculine/feminine, the proportion of both being identical to that of 'Tam O'Shanter'.

So, like Rabbie, I have tried to merge verbal art with mathematics. The marriage of art and science.

APPENDIX II – THE SPIRITUALITY OF
BRAINHEART

Late yestreen, I saw a stranger,
I brought him in.
I put food in the place of the eating,
Drink in the place of the drinking,
Music, song and story in the place of the listening
And the stranger then blessed my beloved ones and my cattle
As the lark sings in her song in the morning
Tis often, often, often goes the Christ in the guise of the stranger.

St Columba's Celtic Rune

Language, racial identity, religion, culture and royalty are the areas that best help indicate the underlying spiritual influence which can be seen in this account of Scotland's geniuses.

LANGUAGE

Coming from Ireland to Scotland, aided by Pictish converts, who were familiar with the Gaelic language, St Columba *(Colm Cille)* began the evangelisation of the native people of Alba from 563AD. The native people spoke a language belonging to the 'P' Celtic languages which was also probably the same language spoken by their near neighbours, the *Breatanaich,* or the Britons. No nationalist therefore need shun the word 'Britain' from an ethnic or geographical standpoint. An eminent Irish Gaelic scholar colleague of mine has unveiled the fact that this ancient word might well be derived from the word *Bruithinn* (Gaelic *Cruithinn*) meaning Pict!

However, the name Britain was to later become synonymous with the economic, political and military union, post 1603/1707. The Gaelic language, on the other hand, belongs to the 'Q' branch of the Celtic languages and came from Ireland with those Scots.

During the glorious days of the Celtic Church, the Gaelic language, together with its customs and beliefs, represented the dominant ethic of all of Scotland and indeed parts of the north of England. But with the receding of the culture of the Gael, including their clan system, the new language of the Anglo Saxon came into Scotland by way of the south-east, together with the Anglo-Norman lairds and the feudal ethic.

When the Scots, or Lallans, tongue replaced Gaelic in the Lowlands, its people were still called Scots. Their new tongue was linguistically Anglo-Saxon in its structure and etymology, containing added Flemish and Norse vocabulary on the eastern seaboard's dialects, and Gaelic loan words in the west. However, it still remained overtly Celtic in its sentiment, in the expression of its poetry, song and story. The *Mither Tongue* is yet couthy, hearty, embracing long lost kinship and above all, it is kind. It is endearing and speaks not to the mind but to the heart. It has taken the wise in their own foolishness. Its language and Celtic perspective marches on yet in our times.

RACIAL IDENTITY

When it comes to racial identity, the terms 'Scots' and 'Scottish' are often freely used interchangeably, with reference to race or of the place of one's origin. For the purpose of *Brainheart,* I would like to suggest that the term 'Scottish' might be used in reference to someone simply born in Scotland, irrespective of their own racial/ethnic background, whereas the term 'Scots' would suggest a genealogical pedigree, not necessarily depicting place of birth, but place of family or name origin.

I would like at this point to further say that I do not believe that there is such a thing as a pure race, with regard to bloodline alone. Therefore, when I use the term 'race' or 'nation', I am referring to the combinations of various. Those factors would certainly include names, genealogy and kinship; but also language, philosophy, spirituality/religion, ethnology, ethics, geography, topography, customs and manners of living, diet, modes of warfare, domestic and national economy, prominent occupational lifestyles, climate, dress, native artistic expression, i.e. music, stories, poems, songs and other forms of verbal wisdom such as proverbs. And, most of all, the way they perceive their womenfolk.

Some Scots have recently deemed it expedient to suggest that the original Scots were not an Irish race at all, as with the highlighting of inconclusive 'archaeological' findings. Recent comparative DNA tests have proved what the Gaelic hereditary custodians of the genealogies and the clan lore (the *Seannachaidhs*) to be correct. Those artisans may have embellished the history, but most certainly would never have fabricated it. The original Scots (with a strong Greek infusion), came from Northern Spain by way of Ireland.

RELIGION

By the time Kenneth McAlpin gained the throne in 843AD, Christianity had been well established for at least a century, all over the kingdom from the Solway Firth to John O'Groats.

When missionaries first came from Ireland, they brought with them an early form of Christianity that exuded forgiveness, mercy and compassion, for those who might respond. They knew no dread of the future nor damnation.

This golden age would last until its incarceration and ultimate fossilisation from the reign of Malcolm Canmore's now canonised wife, Margaret. Scotland's heritage of architectural relics and denominational 'churchianity' lays testimony to this. Its hierarchic legacy echoes on. With its event-determined repetitions, how could they hope to meet spiritual needs that are so fundamental to the yearning of the human soul? An old Hindu/Christian convert said 'there is too much "Christianity" in the world and not enough of Christ!' How true.

St Columba died in 597AD. Exactly one century after this, the monks of Iona were drafting a constitution of human rights, the first ever in history. In the year 800AD, they were penning out the first written legal constitution in Europe, with all its human rights. It was to be re-echoed throughout ages to come, by various monarchs, politicians, reformers, missionaries, founders of political thought, movements and, indeed, founders of new countries or states such as the USA and indirectly, the Chinese Republic. Whether these movements were of the so-called left or right wings, their founders, promoters and activists were to retain that inherent, although perhaps unconscious, Celtic humanity, common to them all.

With the Anglicisation of the Celtic Church, through the marriage of Malcolm Canmore to Princess Margaret of England, came its demise, the demise of its court, and of Gaelic as being its official and legal language. The enactment's commanding lairds producing feudal charters for 'their' land was to follow soon after. This alien feudal ethic of 'people over property' was to be another notch in the gradual downfall of our society. But even throughout the Reformation and beyond, the people of Scotland retained a Celtic consciousness. I believe that this was, and still is, true of the Gael, but nevertheless, it is yet visible with the Lowland Scot.

The old non-exclusive, egalitarian Celtic Church came with its inherent and doctrinal code of hospitality, whose grace and mercy would make room for the stranger to be cordially embraced and protected when under your roof and into your heart and hearth. This legacy is overtly traceable back to Oriental spirituality, which the first Christianity came from. Embers of Eastern spiritual perspective within Scottish indigenous art are still evident, even in modern lingual and musical expression.

In the *Gaidhealtachd* such benevolence would have been extended to your guest(s) even supposing they might have recently been your opponent on the field of battle. Such was the code of mutual honour, that up until the end of the Highland Hero age, it was not uncommon to find inscribed on the blades of Highland swords: *Draw me not without cause and sheathe me not without honour.*

As an Army Intelligence Officer during World War II, whilst interrogating German prisoners in the desert, Hamish Henderson utilised a very effective and simple technique of gaining cooperation from his prisoners: singing him one of his own German folk songs, and tell him his own nation's traditional stories. (The Nazi's Ministry of Propaganda suppressed Germans' native culture and re-wrote German songs, history and identity.) He told some of them more about their own culture than they might have known themselves. The confidence of the prisoner won, Hamish then proceeded to show him the 'error of his ways'. Their cooperation was rewarded by reasonable treatment as prisoner-of-war in Britain. This was a mutually beneficial relationship. Although they were prisoners in his custody during this period, they were still 'a' the Bairns o' Adam' (a phrase from Hamish's great song 'Freedom Come All Ye', which almost became a national, and indeed an international, anthem).

When Hamish died, further revelations of his background began to emerge. Notably, one of them was the fact that his real father was the cousin of the Duke of Atholl, therefore revealing a royal pedigree, through the line of the Stewarts, back to King Robert the Bruce himself. He successfully managed to conceal this, as he felt that it might stand in his way. This was something that others perhaps might have tried to 'cash in on', but not Hamish. Hamish understood a great truth – that rank and authority are for the purpose of servitude.

The 'Guid Man o' Ballangeich' worked in the fields with the folk, he introduced the minimum wage, he dressed as a packman in order to hear what the people really had to say, he made contact with people on the ground who 'knew things'. That man was James v.

ROYALTY

The Stewarts, hailing back to their more remote Celtic ancestors, promoted education for all, in a golden age where Scotland, as an independent nation, traded with France, Spain, Portugal and any-one they wanted to, and on their own terms. This resulted in a very European-orientated cosmopolitanism, which has never yet been repeated unto this day. We even then ate as healthily as the French did, whose wine was our national drink! Many of the coastal people could speak a number of languages and indeed, the better-to-do ones had their education polished in those places. The independent Scots crown and government empowered peo-ple. It's no wonder therefore, that such a small nation on a world scale could produce so many geniuses, so far out of proportion to its population. Unlike people of some other nations, the Scots – Highland and Lowland – were a people tied by blood.

Mary Queen of Scots lived just along the road from the out-spoken reformer, John Knox, who suffered no hint of Spanish Inquisitional-type retribution from her. Queen Mary decreed that all people should worship in whichever way they chose.

Mary did this by issuing an edict of religious toleration – the first in Great Britain. Throughout her career she showed remarkable clemency and lack of bigotry towards her citizens of a different religion, marking her out from almost all her contemporaries.

Was Mary perhaps unconsciously a Celtic Christian?

Perhaps if Mary had been allowed to, she might have proved to be the most progressive queen Europe had ever known at that time. Scotland might have been a model state and example to the rest of the world to follow on human rights, freedom of worship, thought and expression. Under Mary's stewardship, a pattern might have been set to avoid the 'Mickey Fin' of 'divide and rule' wile, which our ancient enemy was to slip us.

Mary's inherent integrity, honesty, innocence and honour betrayed her. I believe that Mary's crossing the border and look-ing to her cousin for help in time of need allegorically represents England's 'guardianship' of Scotland.

King James vi of Scotland and i of England was to introduce to England what had been sown in Scotland from its foundation, i.e.

the right for people to have direct access to the Scripture. His reign oversaw the re-translation of the Hebrew and Greek texts of the Holy Bible, at the direction of George Buchanan of Killearn. This masterpiece of western literature allowed people of low estate throughout Britain to have access to the foundational doctrine of Christianity and meant that they no longer necessarily had to be at the mercy of hierarchic censorship, or subject to the winds of dynastic sectarian change. This development was truly revolutionary for ordinary people's rights in its time.

Much later, in the reign of George II, Alexander Cruden's (7) first ever Concordance to the Holy Bible and Dictionary of the Scriptures would further aid, augment and deepen people's understanding of what the Scriptures declared.

James VII/II was to pass an Act of Parliament in England in 1685, which would reflect Mary and her people's broadmindedness. But that Act, with its democracy for Scotland and religious liberty for all, was too far ahead of its time and totally alien to the thinking of the Puritan hierarchy in London. The 1685 Act echoed once more those most ancient rights penned by the Celtic monks of Iona, many centuries before. The movement was to be called the Jacobite movement. But the Puritans got rid of James and replaced him with a non-Celtic ascendancy. The Scots had been robbed of one of their most precious jewels, i.e. the right to be. King James VII's Act of 1685 is regarded in the USA as the blueprint of the Human Rights Movement.

Some historians have suggested that King James VII's persecution of the Convenanters was because of their Presbyterianism, but was that the case? Or were the noble Covenanters, conned by the ignoble Cromwell into thinking that they shared the same goal, which was to result in the illegal killing of his father? Might it have been for that reason that he held them with distrust? Shortly before this the great Covenanter and Royalist, James Graham, the Marquis of Montrose, attempted to re-marry the concept of 'King and Parliament' together, 'rendering to Caesar that which was Caesar's and to God that which was God's'.

It is from Cromwell's intrusions into Scotland that we owe much of our divide and rule, Sabbatarianism, sectarianism, religious judgmental and legalistic constrictions, which were most certainly to be established with the coming of the Williamite and Hanoverian administrations. Their Anglo-colonial policy was to be enforced in the New World.

In America, the Scots Gael Angus MacKay (*Aonghas MacAoidh*) of Rhode Island, who was a great advocate of the Gaelic language as being inextricably connected with its culture, saw a relationship between England's imperial ambitions over Scotland and the Puritans' genocide past. He connected this to racism in both North America and Britain, thus demonstrating empathy with the Native Americans.

Those Puritan alien ideologies were to corrupt what was, I believe, a very liberal Reformation from which, in the Lowlands, much of the inspiration for innovation came. And yet for all this, even to date, poor John Knox still carries all the blame for Cromwell's spiritual thuggery, which was to come a century after the start of the Reformation. Unlike the true Biblical 'Liberty of Christ', Cromwell's pseudo-Christian sentiment tried to impose a spirit of gloom over Scottish native Celtic psyche, which had previously known no fear of the future. Cromwell's doctrine and subsequent 'Hanoverian' religion did not take a foothold in the Highlands until about a century after Culloden. For all that, the Scot managed to retain that Celtic spark.

CONCLUSION

I would suggest that the Reformation and Covenanting movement for the most part re-opened the floodgates for free thought in the Lowlands, as did the Jacobite movement in the Gaelic-speaking Highlands. Yet the question remains – without the demise of the non-hierarchic Celtic Church, would either movements have been necessary?

Those human rights movements would serve each society within Scotland, according to their respective cultures. Some Covenanting families also became Jacobites, yet remained Covenanters. These movements, I believe, were attempts by both societies within Scotland to try and piece together fragments of what was long lost for the nation as a whole.

With the passing of the Alien and Navigation Act of 1704 and 1705, forbidding Scotland to trade with its ancient European partners as well as America, combined with the failure of the Darien scheme, the country was bankrupted through sanctions into an economic and political union in 1707 that it had been doing its best to resist. Scotland, I believe, was not sold out by treason, but by starvation.

All of this economic, social and political pressure squeezed to the top what was already lying unconsciously dormant in what was once a truly spiritual people, manifesting itself in a great liberty and generosity of heart, fealty, thriftiness, stewardship, daring, irrepressible courage, wit, wisdom, and above all, humanitarianism. This was all grown from that most sacred foundation, making a totally unique race that we call the Scots. As the Greeks were the innovators of the ancient world, so the Scots are with the new.

APPENDIX III — NOVA-RIDDLES

Below are 16 of my 41 original nova-riddles, i.e. riddles concerning Scottish inventions.

The 16 riddles here reflect inventions by innovators in this volume. The answers are on the next page.

1

Black is the stuff
That burns your souls
Marshmallow in sun
And toffee in snow

2

Its upon a browned mat I lie
Frae roon' the world I hingit high
Appeal to taste for all to buy
Frae Dundee toon, a toast for aye

3

It coddles me close
When I hear hear pitter patter
On models I've posed
I'm no fear't o' the watter

4

It sticks in the corner night and day
And from that neuk it does not stray
Yet round the world it will gae
But in that corner there to stay

5

Like merry dancers bright and trim
We'll set; advance around the rim
You'll come and spy us out and in
dance through a circus long and thin

6

As brook without stones
I sing only one note
I look just like drones
Round yer roof like a mote

7

A hall of mirrors for the sky
In northern lights begun
Beholding worlds for you and I
Uncovering nights from sun

8

It's on two steel legs
My sleepers lie
In tunnels hoot real well
On steep parts sigh.

9

I'm a bright onion that
Will ne'er mak' ye weep
For I keep in my skin a' the day
I've a right sunny hat
And I'll hassle and greet ye frae sleep
In the place waur ye lay.

10

It's a yarn tae me
It's a yarn tae you
As through the eye I go
I canna yet see
I am no yet true:
Ye tied me in a bow

11

Shanks Pony there came
Great cone, white and stout
Grand throne wi' a chain
Shanks Pony came out *

12

Wi right cauld taes
For feet on flair
Kirk-a-day
And not a hair.

13

Burling blades
Blunted blazing
Bursting base
Bludgeoning baring

14

Transported to transcend
Taking on the tippler
Transformed to truly tempt
Tables o' toff and tinkler. * *

15

Great groves that grew
As storeys shew
ae e-en sae brave 'n' wanton
In droves hae flew
sae old tae new
fae Reekie tae Manhattan

16

It's my forte
The stripes are laid
In *'broad wood'* fair an' lang.
I'll while away
An' *'list'* aa day
In guid mood wi' the sang

* Very tricky
** The clue is in the nova-riddle 15 times.

Answers to the Nova-riddles

1. Tar, 2. Marmalade, 3. Raincoat, 4. Postage stamp,
5. Kaleidoscope, 6. Drainage guttering, 7. Mirror telescope,
8. Steam power (train), 9. Light bulb, 10. Cotton thread,
11. The water closet (Shanks, Barrhead eventually became the
brand-name), 12. Lawnmower, 13. Linoleum, 14. Tea,
15. Skyscrapers, 16. The Grand Piano

FURTHER READING

Adam, F, *The Clans, Septs and Regiments of the Scottish Highlands* (Johnston and Bacon, 1984)

Bathurst, B, *The Lighthouse Stevensons* (Harper Collins, 1999)

Bennett, Margaret, *Scottish Customs from the Cradle to the Grave* (Polygon, 1992)

Black, Ronald, *An Lasair – Anthology of 18th Century Gaelic Verse* (Birlinn Ltd, 2001)

Bullinger. E.W., *The Companion Bible – the Authorised Version of 1611 with Structures and Critical and Explanatory Notes* (Samuel Bagster & Sons Ltd, 1974 ed.)

Burns, Robert, *The Complete Poems and Songs of Robert Burns* (Geddes & Grosset, 2004 ed)

Burt, Edmund, *Burt's Letters from the North of Scotland* (Birlinn Ltd, 1998)

Campbell, J.F., *Sgeulachdan Ghaidhealach – Popular Tales of the West Highlands Volumes I – IV* (Edmonston and Douglas, 1860)

Chambers, *Scottish Biographical Dictionary* (W & R Chambers Ltd, 1993)

Clan Gregor Society, *Newsletter, Number 58, Winter 2004*

Cruden, Alexander, *Cruden's Complete Concordance to the Old and New Testaments* (Lutterworth Press 1934 ed)

Freeman. James M, *Manners and Customs of the Bible* (Logos International, 1972 ed)

Gibson, John S, *Locheil of the '45'* (Edinburgh University Press, 1994)

Grant, I.F., *Highland Folk Ways* (Birlinn Ltd, 1995)

Hamilton of Gilbertfield, *Blind Harry's Wallace* (Luath Press, 1998 ed)

Heaney, Marie, *Over Nine Waves (A book of Irish legends)* (Faber & Faber, 1994)

Henderson, Hamish, *Hamish Henderson, Collected Poems and Songs* (Curly Snake Publishing, 2000)

Horsburgh, David, *Gaelic and Scots in Grampian* (Aberdeen University Celtic Society, 1994)

Hunter, James, *Scottish Highlanders, Indian Peoples* (Mo
Historical Society Press, 1996)

Lorne, Marquis of, *Canada, 100 years ago* (Bracken Book
1985 ed)

MacColl, Ewan & Seeger, Peggy., *Travellers' Songs from
England & Scotland* (Routledge, 1977)

Mackenzie, Alexander, *History of the Munros of Foulis*
(A & W Mackenzie, 1853)

MacInnes, Dr John, *The Panegyric Code in Gaelic Poetry*
(Transactions of the Gaelic Society of Inverness Volume 1,
1978)

MacLeod, Donald, *Gloomy Memories of the Highlands of
Scotland* (B. Jain Publishers Ltd, 1841 & 1921 ed)

MacLeod, Isabeal, *The Illustrated Encyclopaedia of Scotland*
(Lomond Books, 2004)

Marshall, J.O.C., *Dalriada, A Guide around the Celtic Kingdo*
(Glenarrif Development Group, 1998)

McNeill, Marian F., *The Scots Kitchen* (Blackie & Sons Ltd,
1968 ed)

McNeill, Marian F., *The Scots Cellar* (Richard Paterson,
1956 ed)

McNeill, Marian F., *The Silver Bough* (Canongate Publishing,
1989 ed)

Murray W.H., *Rob Roy MacGregor, His Life and Times*
(Richard Drew Publishing, 1982)

Neat, Timothy & MacInnes, John, *The Voice of the Bard*
(Canongate, 1999)

Skene, W.F., *Celtic Scotland. Volume I, History and Ethnology*
(David Douglas, 1886)

Skene, W.F., *Celtic Scotland. Volume II, Church and Culture*
(David Douglas, 1887)

Skene, W.F., *Celtic Scotland. Volume III, Law and People*
(David Douglas, 1880)

Stewart, Douglas, *MacTalla, Echoes of Our Ancestral Past*
(1974)

Wills, Elspeth, *Scottish Firsts* (Mainstream Publishing Company
Ltd, 2002)

INDEX

Aberdeen 7, 28
Aberdeen (county) 3
Abolition of Moorish piracy 15
Adhesive postage stamp 38
Air doorbell 18
Alaska 43
Alba (Scotland) 5
Albain (Scotland) 12
Algebra's convergent series 2
Allegheny Mountains (USA) 23
Alloway, Ayrshire 19
America (see USA) 1, 14
America's first architect 8
America's first geology map 23
America's independence signatory 9
Antarctic 45
Antarctica claimed for Queen
    Victoria 45
Anthems for all mankind 19
Appalachia 41
Aral Sea 41
Arbroath 9, 29, 38, 46
Arbuthnot, John 3
Arch Street, Philadelphia 8
Arctic 24, 27
Asia 41
Assam 49
Atlantic 23, 26, 45
Auckland Isles 45
Auld Reekie (see Edinburgh) 2, 8,
    9, 12, 16, 17, 21, 29, 32, 50
Australia 22, 36
Automated dry cleaning 47
Ayr 23
Ayrshire 25
Ballochmyle 19
Baltic 41
Bannockburn 19
Barra, Isle of 24
Bears brought back to Perthshire
    41
Beith 9
Bell Rock lighthouse 29
Bell Rock, Arbroath 29

Bennett, James Gordon 42
Bergen 1
Berlin 5
Berwick 49
Bethnal Green (London) 7
Billingsport (New Jersey) 8
Birmingham 18
Black slavery abolished in
    Morocco 15
Blackfriars (Perth) 47
Bombay 22, 28
Boothia Gulf 33
Boothia Gulf/Peninsula 33
Boothia Peninsula 33
Brewster, Sir David 35
Bridgewater (Manchester) 50
Britain 14, 15, 20, 40
Broadwood, John 11
Buffalo introduced to Perthshire 41
Burns, Robert 19
Burt's Close (Perth) 47
Caithness 17
Caledonian Canal 21
Campbell Isles 45
Canada 24
Canton crepe, non-imported 30
Cape Horn 43
Carolina 15, 26
Central heating 13
Centrifugal governor 13
Chalmers, James 38
Chief of the Cherokee nation 39
Chief of the Creek Indian Nation
    20
China 30, 49
Chrono-astrolabe 44
Clyde 5, 27, 40
Clyde ship-building, father of 40
Coats, James 30
Cockburnspath 11
Cockspur 18
Coddington Lense 35
Concordance to the Bible 7
Consultant chemist, first ever 34

Consultant engineer, world's first
  21
Cornwall 18
Cota Canal (Sweden) 21
Cotton thread 30
Crimea 41
Cromdale 28
Cruden, Alexander 7
Culloden 20, 27
Cumming, Alexander 32
Dalkeith Park 8
Dalrymple, Sir Hugh 6
Darjeeling 49
Dee (side) 2
Delaware River (USA) 8
Dictionary of the Scriptures 7
Diffraction grating 2
Douglas, David 43
Douglas fir tree 43
Doune Castle 9
Drainage systems/guttering 6
Drumoak 2
Dublin 28
Dumbarton 40
Dumfries 21
Dundee 16, 31, 38, 44, 48
Dunmaglass 20
Dunvegan 23
Eaton Place, London 41
Edinburgh or Auld Reekie 2, 8, 9,
  12, 16, 17, 21, 29, 32, 50
Egypt 22, 28
Eigg, Isle of 24
Empire (British) 49
England 3, 23, 40
English Channel 33
Europe 15, 23, 40
Fairmount, (Philadelphia) 8
Falconer, Hugh 49
Falkirk 9
Ferguslie, Paisley 30
Ferryport, Fife 16
Field Marshal to Fredrick the
  Great 5
Fife 4, 35, 40
Fire engine 13

First European to climb the
  Rockies 43
First Indian nation to have a
  written language 39
First legally ratified American
  Indian nation 39
First nation founded on
  Christianity Prologue
Flexible drive shaft 50
Foramen of Monro (brain's
  nervous system) 12
Forres 49
Fort Fork (Canada) 24
Forth, River 40
Founding father of Australia 22
France 3, 14, 23, 31, 40
Fraser River (Canada) 24, 43
Gas lighting 18
Gasometer 13
Georgia Russia 41
Georgia (USA) 39
Gibraltar 15
Gibraltar kept British 15
Glasgow 17, 27, 29, 34, 40, 49
Glencoe 3
Glenstrae (Argyll) 39
Gloag, Helen 15
Good Hope, Cape of 45
Governor of the Ukraine 5
Grand piano 11
Grantully Castle 41
Greenock 13
Gregory, James 2
Haddington 9
Hakkim 49
Hand drills 50
Hawaii 43
Hebrides 24
Highway, USA's first 25
Himalayas 49
Hobart (Tasmania) 45
Hochkirk 5
Holyhead 21
Horse power 13
Human rights charter, the world's
  first The Prologue

Humane colonial prison reform
   22, 36
Hydraulic press 50
Inch (Wigtonshire) 33
India 49
India tea 49
Indians brought back to
   Perthshire 41
Inflatable bed 27
Intermittent flashing lights 29
Inverbervie 3
Inverness 20
Ireland 21
Jarvisfield, Mull 22
Jedburgh 35, 37
Jib crane 29
John's Brown's Shipyard (Clyde)
   40
Jones, John Paul 14
Kaleidoscope 35
Keiller, Janet and James 31
Keith 42
Keith, James Francis Edward 5
Key cutter 50
Killiecrankie 3
King William Island 33
Kingsession, Pennsylvania 26
Kinnoul (Perth) 47
Kirkcaldy 10, 48
Kirkcudbright 6, 14
Laid Burn (Perth) 47
Largo 4
Latent heat 34
Law of polarisation of bi-axial
   crystals 35
Lawn mower 46
Leine River, Germany 30
Leith 36
Lewis, Isle of 24
Life-jacket 27
Light-bulb, electric 44
Lighthouse dynasty 29
Lindsay, James Bowman 44
London 11, 18, 23, 32, 34, 36,
   38, 41, 50
Lords Cricket Ground (England)
   46

Loughton 8
Lugar (Ayrshire) 18
MacGillivray, Alexander 20
MacGregor River (Canada) 24
MacGrigor, Sir James 28
Macintosh, Charles 27
Mackenzie, Sir Alexander 24
MacLure, William 23
Maconochie, Alexander 36
MacQuarrie, Lachlan 22
Magnetic North and South Pole
   33, 45
Magnetic North Pole (co-charted)
   33
Manhattan 8
Marishal College 3
Marmalade 31
Maryland (USA) 14
Massachusetts 1
McAdam, John Loudon 25
Mechanisms of the Heavens 37
Med or Mediterranean 33
Menai Straights (Wales) 21
Metrology 34
Mirror telescope 2
Modern journalism 42
Mogador, Morocco 15
Mogador's Port opened for
   European trade 15
Monro, Alexander (Secundus) 12
Montreal 24
Moscow 5
Mull 22
Murdoch, William 18
Murthly Castle 41
Muthill (Perthshire) 15
Nairn, Michael 48
Nairn's Folly (Kirkcaldy) 48
Napier, Robert 40
Nasmyth, James 50
New Harmony (Indiana) 23
New Jersey 9
New Lanark 23
New plant species brought to
   Scotland 43
New South Wales 22
New World (USA) 1, 9, 10, 42, 43

New York 22, 24, 25, 42
New York Herald 42
Newfoundland 1
Newport (USA) 1
North Alberta 24
North Carolina 39
North Pole (magnetic) 33, 45
Northfolk Island (Australia) 36
Northwest Passage (Canada) 24, 33
Norway 1
Nova Scotia 1, 14
Nut-milling 50
Oak Island 1
Ohio 41
Oklahoma 39
Oregon 41
Oregon Trail, pioneer 41
Orkney 1
Ornithologist, America's father of 26
Oxford 37
Paisley 9, 26, 30
Parabolic reflectors 29
Paris 40
Pathhead Sands (Kirkcaldy) 48
Patterned coloured linoleum 48
Peace River (Canada) 24
Penecontaglossal Dictionary 44
Pennsylvania 26
Pentland 1
Perth 47
Perthshire 41
Peterhead 5
Philadelphia 8
Photocopier 13
Planet wheel 18
Pneumatic lift 18
Political economist, first ever 10
Pontcysyllte 21
Portugal 28, 31
President of the Board of Agriculture, first 17
President's House (New Jersey) 8
Princeton College (New Jersey) 8, 9
Probability statistics 3

Prospect Hill 1
Prussia 5
Pullar, John 47
Pyrenees 28
Rabat 15
Raincoat 27
Redruth (Cornwall) 18
Reekie (Auld) 35
Reflector lamps for lighthouses 16
Rhode Island 1
Robinson Crusoe, the real 4
Rockies, Northern 43
Roe, River (Ireland) 12
Ross, James Clark 45
Ross, John (Cherokee) 39
Ross, Sir John 33
Ross Ice Shelf 45
Ross Shelf (Antarctic) 45
Rosslyn (Roslin) 1
Ross-ville 39
Royal Army Medical Corps 28
Royal Astronomical Society, first woman 37
Rum, Isle of 24
Russia 14
Sacramento Valley 43
Safety foundry ladle 50
Saharánpur (India) 49
Salle (Morocco) 15
Scone 43
Scotland 9, 19, 39
Scottish Empress of Morocco 15
Screw propeller 13
Self-adjusting bearings 50
Selkirk, Alexander 4
Semple Castle (Ayrshire) 26
Seville 31
Shanks, Alexander 46
Sherrifmuir 5
Shetland 1
Shropshire 21
Sinclair, Jarl 1
Sinclair, Sir John 17
Slide rule 13
Slide valve 18
Smith, Adam 10

Smith, Robert 8
Smith, Thomas 16
Smoky Mountains (N. Carolina) 39
Somerville, Mary Fairfax 37
Somerville College (Oxford) 37
South Pole, magnetic 45
Spain 20, 28, 41
St Andrew's Greens 46
St Andrews Square (Edinburgh) 29
St Peter's Church (Philadelphia) 8
Stair 6
States (see USA) 23
Statistical account, first ever 17
Steam car 18
Steam hammer 50
Steam power/Industrial revolution 13
Steam, train, ferry 40
Stepps of Russia 41
Stereoscope 35
Stevenson, Robert 29
Stewart, Sir William Drummond 41
Stornoway 24
Sun wheel 18
Surgeon General to Wellington 28
Sweden 33
Switzerland 11
Tabloid newspaper, world's first 42
Tar (mac) 25
Tashkent 41
Tasmania 36
Tay, River, Valley 44
Telford, Thomas 21
Telford New Town 21

The 'Watt' (unit) 13
The English grand action (piano) 11
Thermostat (Bimetal) 34
Thistle Hall (Dundee) 44
Toulouse 28
Trans-Atlantic steamer, first 40
Transmitting messages through seawater 44
Tulloch (Perth) 47
Turkey 41
USA 20
USA's Navy founder 14
Ukraine 5
Ulva 22
Ure, Andrew 34
Vacuum coffee machine 40
Vancouver 43
Venice 1
Victoria Barrier (Antarctic) 45
Virginia 23
Vitoria 28
Washington 39, 42
Water closet 32
Waterloo 28, 41
Watt, James 13
West Indies 28
West Pacific Ocean 24
Westerkirk 21
Westminster Abbey 38
Wick 1
Wigton 33
Wilson, Alexander 26
Witherspoon, John 9
Written legal constitution, first in Europe Prologue
Yester 9

Some other books published by **LUATH** PRESS

Luath Storyteller: Tales of the Picts

Stuart McHardy
ISBN 1 84282 097 4 PBK £5.99

For many centuries the people of Scotland have told stories of their ancestors, a mysterious tribe called the Picts. This ancient Celtic-speaking people, who fought off the might of the Roman Empire, are perhaps best known for their Symbol Stones – images carved into standing stones left scattered across Scotland, many of which have their own stories. Here for the first time these tales are gathered together with folk memories of bloody battles, chronicles of warriors and priestesses, saints and supernatural beings. From Shetland to the Border with England, these ancient memories of Scotland's original inhabitants have flourished since the nation's earliest days and now are told afresh, shedding new light on our ancient past.

Luath Storyteller: Highland Myths & Legends

George W Macpherson
ISBN 1 84282 064 8 PBK £5.99

The mythical, the legendary, the true – this is the stuff of stories and storytellers, the preserve of Scotland's ancient oral tradition.

Celtic heroes, fairies, Druids, selkies, sea horses, magicians, giants, Viking invaders – all feature in this collection of traditional Scottish tales, the like of which have been told around campfires for centuries and are still told today.

Drawn from storyteller George W Macpherson's extraordinary repertoire of tales and lore, each story has been passed down through generations of oral tradition – some are over 2,500 years old. Strands of these timeless tales cross over and interweave to create a delicate tapestry of Highland Scotland as depicted by its myths and legends.

I have heard George telling his stories... and it is an unforgettable experience... This is a unique book and a 'must buy'...

DALRIADA: THE JOURNAL OF CELTIC HERITAGE AND CULTURAL TRADITIONS

Luath Press Limited
committed to publishing well written books worth reading

LUATH PRESS takes its name from Robert Burns, whose little collie Luath (*Gael.*, swift or nimble) tripped up Jean Armour at a wedding and gave him the chance to speak to the woman who was to be his wife and the abiding love of his life. Burns called one of 'The Twa Dogs' Luath after Cuchullin's hunting dog in Ossian's *Fingal*. Luath Press was established in 1981 in the heart of Burns country, and is now based a few steps up the road from Burns' first lodgings on Edinburgh's Royal Mile.

Luath offers you distinctive writing with a hint of unexpected pleasures.

Most bookshops in the UK, the US, Canada, Australia, New Zealand and parts of Europe either carry our books in stock or can order them for you. To order direct from us, please send a £sterling cheque, postal order, international money order or your credit card details (number, address of cardholder and expiry date) to us at the address below. Please add post and packing as follows: UK – £1.00 per delivery address; overseas surface mail – £2.50 per delivery address; overseas airmail – £3.50 for the first book to each delivery address, plus £1.00 for each additional book by airmail to the same address. If your order is a gift, we will happily enclose your card or message at no extra charge.

Luath Press Limited
543/2 Castlehill
The Royal Mile
Edinburgh EH1 2ND
Scotland
Telephone: 0131 225 4326 (24 hours)
Fax: 0131 225 4324
email: sales@luath.co.uk
Website: www.luath.co.uk